EDEN
ENFORCER

STEPHANIE HUDSON

Eden's Enforcer
Lost Siren Series #2
Copyright © 2022 Stephanie Hudson
Published by Hudson Indie Ink
www.hudsonindieink.com

Eden's Enforcer/Stephanie Hudson – 1st ed.
ISBN-13 - 978-1-913904-23-4

I would like to dedicate this book to Claire L Monaghan,
Author of the Midnight Gunn series.
A lady, who's strength utterly astounds me and who selfless acts
towards others reminds you every day the true nature of
kindness and humanity. Claire went through breast cancer and
after experiencing all that Cancer can do to a person's life and
family, she came out the other side wanting only to help others.
She founded the Steel Petals name and published the book,
Steel Petals Voices: Poems that speak a thousand words.
All proceeds raised under the Steel Petals name go to different
Cancer charities and the book features poems by others that
have been affected by the disease.
I consider myself privileged to know Claire and am honoured to
have the gift of her words in my book...

Journey is a dirty word

A journey full of pain and fear
Is not a journey I revere.
This journey, isolated and alone
Is not a journey I condone.

Journey is a dirty word
In suffering company, rest assured.

Forced upon a road less travelled
Struggling, choices momentarily shackled.

Oh, unwanted companion
Journey is a dirty word.

-C. L. Monaghan
Author ©2021

CHAPTER I
CALLING A HERO'S NAME
EDEN

"WARD!" I screamed his name the second I saw him emerging from the door I had just been dragged through, knowing that any second now he would save me!

Because that's what he did.

He was my Hero.

"NOW! FUCKING BLOW IT... NOW, GOD DAMN IT!" I heard these words and cried out,

"NOOOO!" But it was too late. The man I loved was suddenly consumed in an explosion of glass and concrete, making me slap a hand to the window as who had quickly become my whole world went up in flames.

"Ward... no... it can't be... it..." I whispered in my grief and my heart felt as if it had been ripped wide open! I felt myself being pulled backwards and in the midst of my agony, I let them, knowing that now I no longer gave a shit what happened to me.

Because if Ward wasn't in my world, then there was no world worth living in. I knew it sounded crazy, seeing as I hadn't known him for more than a few days, but I didn't care!

1

I had fallen in love regardless.

The type of love I knew a person didn't have a hope of ever getting over. Which meant the fight I once had for survival had gone up in smoke, just as that building did now. The one I could still see burning. The explosion had been enough that it rocked the van from its wheels and every time a bigger piece of it crumbled down, you felt the vibrations from where it landed. In fact, it was hard to see much more than the blackened mushroom clouds of smoke that bellowed up into the night. But the sounds, I would never forget. The sound of glass smashing. The sound of walls cracking. The sound of the metal twisting as the fire escape fell from the concrete it had once been anchored to.

And of course...

The sounds of my own screaming as each new piece of the building fell on the now mangled body of the man I loved.

But then, just as the van started to turn a corner, doing so at speed, the guy in the front seat, who was now ripping his chef whites off, barked down the phone once more.

"Blow the second one, Finch, do it before this fucker gets too close." I quickly turned to look and ended up crying out as I saw Ward's car coming for us. I could then briefly see Deke driving before I was once again screaming. Because just before he could get too close, it too blew up! The explosion was so powerful that it threw both the car up from its tires and Deke from the shattering glass windshield.

"NO! Fuck no, you fucking bastards!" I screamed, as they didn't just take Ward but his best friend! At this I turned quickly and attacked, scratching my nails down one guy's face, feeling the sick satisfaction that they did enough damage that I felt blood dripping from them.

"Fucking Bitch!" This was the last thing I heard before the blissful silence of unconsciousness took away my heartache as I was punched across the face. It was hard enough that I passed out before my head hit the floor of the van.

And for once...

I welcomed the pain.

❧

The next time I woke fully, it was to find myself upright and now unable to move. I'd had fleeting moments of awareness before this point, like feeling as if my body was being manhandled and obviously moved to where the bad guys wanted me. But it was the slamming of some shutter doors that finally jerked me back into my situation. However, the first thing that hit me, wasn't a fist this time but the pain of memory.

"Ward." I muttered his name on a wounded whisper. Whatever injury I had sustained from being hit was nothing compared to the agony of remembering that I had lost him. Because surely, supernatural being or not, *nothing could survive that?*

"Aww look, the little bitch is pining for her dog!" A man's voice sneered before I was slapped around enough to force my attention their way. I gritted my teeth and again welcomed the pain as it gave me something else to focus on instead of my heartbreak, if only for a few seconds. But then, my new dark world started to come back into focus and when opening my eyes, I saw the one who I had attacked. A Hispanic man who now had four angry red lines down one cheek and neck, where I had raked my nails down his face. He was also the one who looked the most pissed off and considering the damage, then it was not surprising he most likely wanted me dead. And what a shit hole to die in. Not that dying in any other place should matter now, as it meant nothing. Not when I had lost everything. So, whether it had been sitting on some beautiful

3

beach, calmly watching as the waves rolled in, or inside this shitty abandoned warehouse, where not even any sunlight would filter through the filth, death was death.

And I had nothing left to live for.

"Yeah, maybe I should stick my dick in her mouth and give her something else to pine over," a man with a shaved head said, one half of which was covered by a tattoo of a spider's web that had a skeletal hand entwined through it. He was also one of the four men I recognized from the van that were now all positioned around me. Two were sitting, one of which included the guy I had left my mark on. Another sitting with his chair turned backward so he could rest his arms across the back part, with a gun held casually in one hand. He was older than the rest, with a thin face and cruel, dark eyes. As for the last one, he was standing close to the doors, obviously on guard duty. He had long messy dark hair tied back into a ponytail with tattoos covering every inch of his neck. Each of them were dressed like your typical bad guy movie extras, except the older guy who was wearing a dark grey suit.

"Try it and you will also find this bitch bites," I told them, thinking I would rather they just outright killed me than come anywhere near me with their dicks!

"Yeah, well that wouldn't do you much good after I first knock all your teeth out!" The bald guy replied with a sneer.

"Eww, fuck Ricky, that's sick even for you," the guy by the door commented.

"A hole is a hole, just so long as I don't get my dick bitten off, then I don't give a fuck where it goes," the bald guy replied, sickening me and making me feel sorry for the rest of the female population just being around this asswipe!

"Well, your dick is staying in your pants for now, as least until we hear word from the boss on when we are to kill this bitch and where he wants the body dumping this time," the thin man in the suit said and at this, I couldn't help but shiver despite being tied up. Seriously, if all they had planned was to kill me, then why not just let me blow up in that building... why not let me die in the arms of the man I loved so we may have gone together. Or was that the point?

Was I to be made an example of?

"Yeah, well I say we just fucking shoot the bitch!" the Hispanic guy said, one who looked to be silently fuming all this time. Oh, and the one who looked as if he had been mauled by a small jungle cat. He also looked to have reached his limit of waiting to put a bullet in my head as he was now on his feet and pulling a large handgun from the back of his jeans. One he then pointed straight at my head.

"Put the gun down, Santiago. You know the boss didn't say to kill her yet," the guy in the suit said, making me wonder if he was the one in charge of these three?

"Then we just say that she tried to run, and we had to put her down," the one I now knew was named Santiago said, obviously rallying for my death in a big way.

"What, by a bullet in the brain at point blank range, think man, Gomez would have our asses!" the one by the doors added.

"I don't give a fuck! Look what this bitch did to my face!" he snarled back, and I almost told him all the other things I would add to it should I ever get the opportunity... that and a baseball bat.

"Yeah, well think of what Gomez will let his dogs do to your face, man! Fuckin' think for once and keep a lid on it!" the man with the ponytail told him, now leaving the door and joining the rest as it was clear the situation was heating up.

"Fine, I won't shoot the bitch, but that doesn't mean I am not owed some payback!" At this he pulled a knife out of a sheath strapped to his thigh and started to bring it to my face.

This naturally made me squirm back as much as I could. He teased the tip of it at my cheek, making me cry out when I felt the pain of it cut me.

"Seriously man, don't be stupid…" Ponytail said while the bald one seemed to be enjoying the scene. But as for the quieter one in the suit, well his eyes just narrowed, before simply saying his name the once. Something I gathered should have been enough,

"Santiago."

"Shut the fuck up! I am fucking owed this!" he snapped back, waving his gun at them as he must have feared the other three may be about to intervene. Ponytail and baldly both held their hands up and started to back away, but the suited guy just watched, barely moving. Oh, and he didn't look happy about it. Santiago turned his attention back to me, now pointing the blade at my cleavage, cutting down the part between my breasts where the material was at its tightest thanks to my dress. One that had definitely seen better days since I first put it on that evening and now, thanks to his blade, showed a near obscene amount of cleavage.

"Now, I wonder what you would look like if I cut off a nipple, or maybe I don't stop there and go for the whole tit, I could lay it on your boyfriend's grave… that is, *when they finally dig him out."* He said this after bringing his face right up close in front of mine, and I couldn't help it when my anger ignited and reacted before I could stop myself.

"Fuck you!" I shouted the second after I reared my head back and butted him in the nose. Pain exploded both in my head and at the top of my breast as the blade nicked me there from his jerked reaction to being hit. He stumbled back, now holding his bleeding nose and a second later, he reacted in a different way.

"Time to die, bitch!" he roared before putting his gun back

in my face and this time, I could see in slow motion as the hammer was cocked back. That was when I knew that this was it.

This was the end.

My only hope was that I was pure enough in my soul that I would end up in the right place so I might see Ward just one more time. But then a phone rang, and I nearly jumped out of my skin at the sound. The man in the suit answered it and with a silent nod to the bald-headed one who was standing the closest, he quickly clamped a hand on Santiago's wrist, stopping him from shooting me. Then I watched as he nodded to someone behind him and the next thing that happened wasn't what I had anticipated.

Because despite a gun going off, I strangely heard my own scream, a sound of fear that would never have come after death. And Gomez had clearly wanted someone dead.

Only this time...

It wasn't me.

CHAPTER 2

UNDERESTIMATED
WARD

F*ury and rage.*

Pure, undiluted fury and rage. That was all I felt the moment I realized my mistake. The moment I had careered through the kitchen like some whirlwind of death and ripped off the fucking door only to find her being taken from me!

But before this crazed rage and vow of damnation, came another emotion, for the moment I scented her fear, it was *stone cold panic.*

I had failed her.

I knew that the moment I saw her hand reaching out to me through the back window, and my name being called desperately from her lips. But one step later and the whole fucking building came down on top of me and I may have been an Angel, but even my vessel needed time to recover from that. Hence why ten minutes later, and just as I was still trying to burst my way through the tons of burning rubble above me, did I feel a hand reach inside and take hold of my arm.

"Fuck me, Ward, but when you make enemies, you don't dick around," Deke commented as soon as my head was clear, making me climb the rest of the way out with his help. Because, like I said, I was a strong fucker but, well even a six-story building being dropped on my fucking head was going to slow me down.

"Ee...ee...nnn!" I tried to shout, stumbling a little as I tried to walk on broken bones that were still taking the time to heal.

"Whoa there, easy okay, you just need to..." I interrupted him after I quickly forced my jaw back into place where it had come dislocated. Then I snarled,

"The car! Why the fuck didn't you follow them!?"

"Hey, you weren't the only one they tried to blow the shit out of, meaning the fucking car is toast and I just came to after my face started to find its way back to being handsome again," Deke replied, making me finally take a better look at him to see he was torn up and covered in blood, obviously still healing from his own injuries. At this I took a deep breath and placed a hand to his shoulder,

"They... fuck, Deke... they fucking took her!" I told him in a pained way he had probably never heard coming from me before. Hence why he clasped his good hand to my shoulder in return and told me sincerely,

"We will get her back or we will die trying... I give you my word, I am with you on this, Brother." I nodded my thanks before we helped each other down the small hill of rubble that had once been a building. I thought on Deke's vow, coming from the only one closest to family as I would ever get until meeting Eden. It was why he had called me Brother. He understood what my Siren meant to me, which was why I knew that he would give his life to save her own... *we both would.*

Because despite what people thought, we could die. And as for me, there was only one place my soul would end up and unfortunately it would not be in the Heaven I was first born. Because what not many knew was how I came to be here in the first place. How my once white glorious wings had turned black, and my heavenly soul had become tainted with the curse of death.

This had been my punishment.

One that if I failed by dying, then my soul would end up in the one place I had sent countless Demons and tainted souls to rot in the depths of where Lucifer would punish them. The hunter would become the hunted, and no amount of Heavenly power I had in this realm would mean shit in Hell. Not when I was stripped of it, leaving nothing but the bare bones of my soul to rot!

But Deke knew this, being one of only two people that did. The other was,

Vincent Draven.

The Angel who had been there at the day of my judgement and the only one who had spoken for me. It was how I was given new meaning for life and how I became the first of the King's Enforcers. Ironic then that I was to be awarded a Siren from the Fates, seeing as they were part of that judgement. One given for my acts of justice against the Gods who I felt had abused their power for their own good.

But that was the thing with Gods.

They were not all holy, righteous, and just.

Hence why I had no other choice but to be reformed into the Angel of Vengeance and Fear, the very words I had used while I had foolishly been trying to kill a God. But of course, it had not all been bad, considering the transition to such a high-ranking Angel, one transformed to the only one of my kind, meant ending up more powerful than I could have imagined.

However, my vessel hadn't quite got the memo with that one, for I should have allowed my other form to take over completely before I found a building on my head! That way I would have been able to fight my way free in seconds, not the

11

agonizing minutes it had taken my body to fix itself enough to do this.

"How the fuck did they manage this?!" he hissed.

"They must have brought the bomb in and hid it just before taking her, as I didn't scent anything before. Nor did I detect any deception so no one was in the building prior to the kidnapping, or I would have been aware," I replied, knowing that I wouldn't have missed anything, not when there was Eden's life to protect.

"That seems very well planned considering they don't know who they are dealing with," Deke said, making a fucking good point.

"Unless they do, after all, I did leave witnesses," I said, now wishing I hadn't been so dead set on sending a message, instead killing them all.

"Yeah, well they obviously didn't know that it would take more than bringing a building down on your ass to get you to die," he replied dryly, making me growl,

"Clearly."

"So, what is the plan here, Ward?" he asked, making me look around at the area, scanning for any innocent life that I knew would have been taken out in the bombing. But after realizing there was no one to save, I listened out for the sound of sirens, knowing that it wouldn't be long before the rescue services were crawling all over this site.

"I know that look," Deke commented in a perceptive tone.

"I have a plan, but it starts back at the hotel... that is if my hunch in right," I told him, now moving our way quickly down the side streets, as the explosion had already started to draw in a crowd. Naturally, I controlled the minds of those who saw us, as we weren't exactly inconspicuous. We both looked like we had dragged our way through this fucking nightmare.

"I have never known your hunches to be wrong before but

then again, I have never known you to get buried alive, either," Deke said, making me snarl back,

"Rome, 1402... the locals thought I was hiding a..."

"A Strix, yes I remember now... I smelled of that horse shit days after digging you out of that field." I scoffed at this, remembering his complaints. The locals had believed I had in my possession a Strix, a creature that the Romans believed was a bird of ill omen, the product of metamorphosis, one that fed on human flesh and blood.

"Irrational mortals will always present themselves, and well, some cultures will always act more foolish than others," I pointed out as we continued to move through the streets.

"You can say that again," he commented dryly and after I raised a brow at him, he added, "The same people that buried you alive, also believed the old superstition that kissing a female mule in the nostrils cured hiccups and a runny nose." I scoffed at the memory as it was true and unfortunately, not the worst one by far.

We picked up pace when the sound of more vehicles approached and I had to wonder how many on Gomez's payroll would be there, quick to pin this down to being a gas leak. Well, it wouldn't matter, for Gomez would soon realize it was insignificant as to how many cop's palms he had greased, nothing would save him from my wrath.

Minutes later, and we were far enough away that I started scanning the street for a suitable vehicle.

"Come on." I nodded and by the time we reached what I was looking for, both our vessels were fully healed and back to being what they were before the destruction.

"At least someone on this street has some taste," Deke said the moment I paused at the brand new yellow and black Chevrolet Camaro SS. Then I closed my eyes a moment and reached out to the mind of the owner who was currently trying to convince his girlfriend to give him a blow job. So, I took hold of his mind, planted the idea that he left his car at the hotel and would not be needing it again for a few days. After all, the last thing I needed was cops to deal with. And well, I needed a fucking car, and a fast one at that.

But this wasn't all I did, as I left him with the urge to selflessly go down on his girlfriend, give her at least three orgasms before the night was done and go to bed without sexual release. This was his punishment for trying to get his girlfriend to do anything she didn't have the energy to do after a twelve-hour shift as a waitress.

After this I unlocked what I knew was his pride and joy, and started it up with only a thought, making the parts move that I knew I needed to. This was done with the kind of energy a supernatural like me could tap into, using it to manipulate practically anything. Say, a starter motor and fuck load of pistons.

After this I floored it back to the hotel and told Deke my plan on the way, knowing what I knew of Felix Gomez...

He had fucked up big time.

But that was what happened when you underestimated your enemy...

You became a Dead Man!

CHAPTER 3

BARGAIN WITH DEATH

"So, this plan of yours?" Deke asked when I pulled close to the hotel but far enough away from it that we wouldn't be seen.

"Relies heavily on them having a back-up plan," I replied before telling him exactly what I wanted. Meaning that when we exited the car, he took a more visible and deliberate route into the front of the hotel. As for me...

I went hunting.

I drew the shadows in around me, masking myself as I waited for what I was looking for. Then, as soon as Deke was seen walking into the hotel, I scanned the people along the street, and the first guy to pull out his phone, I homed in on him. A guy in his late forties, wearing a hooded jacket with the hint of a goatee showing beneath.

Then using my powers, I scented two things...

Sin and explosives.

He started to make his way to a park across from the hotel which would give him a better view of the penthouse window. That was when I knew what he was waiting for, just as I suspected. I waited until he pulled a phone from his jacket pocket and dialed the only number I needed from him.

I continued to stalk him from the shadows, clearing the space around him and making sure no other mortals would get in between me and my prey. Of course, the clueless fuck had no idea just what horror stood waiting to claim his soul, and I swear had it not been for the fact that my girl had been taken, I would have grinned.

But as it was, I was going out of my fucking mind with worry! However, I knew that instead of trying to tear this city apart in an attempt at finding her, there was a quicker way. One that wouldn't mean potentially losing precious time in trying to find her, and therefore taking me straight to the source.

Enter pawn number one.

"Yeah, it's me, Finch... Go tell Gomez that he was right, one of those fuckers just entered the hotel. It looks like he survived the second bomb," the guy said, waiting for his reply before he asked,

"What do you think, dipshit, go ask him what he wants me to do?!" I sneered behind my veil of darkness, just itching to take hold of his neck and snap it like a fucking twig this park was full of. However, I waited as I knew patience would aid me far better than my deadly impulses, and I was right.

"I spoke to Gomez." I heard the reply on the other end of the phone, even from a distance, thanks to my heightened senses.

"And, what's my play?" the one named Finch asked, as if desperate to act.

"Do it and call us back when it's done," was his employer's reply, making him grin up at the penthouse.

"With pleasure," he responded, and his merciless sneer was one I wanted to slice from his face at the evil intent he had toward my second. He flipped his phone shut and slid it back into his pocket. Then, as soon as Deke's figure was seen passing a window in the penthouse I was staying in, the guy pulled a device from his pocket. The second I recognized it to be a remote detonator, was when I acted, doing so with inhuman speed.

I seemingly came out of nowhere, as one second he was pressing down on the cell phone taped to what I could see was a rudimentary device and the next, he was howling in pain as I snapped his wrist, making him drop the detonator into my awaiting palm.

"AHHHH... FUCK!" The guy wailed, making me quickly kick out his knee, breaking it instantly. This made him drop to the floor as I'd planned, so I didn't have to concern myself with chasing some dumb fuck around a park.

"That didn't really go your way, now, did it?" I commented in a dry tone that masked the fact that I wanted to tear this guy apart. Then I watched as Deke stepped from the top floor window and released his wings to slow his decent as he dropped to the alleyway. A pair that I knew would not last long, as was his own curse. Which was why his own pair of wings started off as near blinding white and by the time he hit the ground, they were raven black. He then started to cross to our side of the street and as expected, the guy took one look at Deke and was soon trying to crawl away in desperation. Although, I wasn't surprised as one moment, my second looked like some avenging, heavenly Angel and the next, his black wings dissolved into dripping black oil.

I looked down and the sight made me scoff at the vermin's pitiful attempt at saving his own life.

"I see you found the shit stain," Deke observed disdainfully.

"Give it a minute and that may become quite literal, as he already pissed himself," I replied, making Deke chuckle.

STEPHANIE HUDSON

"Haven't lost your touch, I see." I granted him a wry look before glancing down and curling my lip up in disgust.

"Bring him!" I ordered as way of reply, making Deke reach out and twist his fist into the back of his jacket, dragging the wasteful blood sack of flesh one-handed further into the park and somewhere I wasn't forced to control so many minds.

"I assume you found their back up?" I asked, making Deke throw the guy to the ground before answering,

"Exactly as you said there would be." Just then, his phone started ringing, making me grin.

"And right on time." I nodded down at the whimpering, broken and bleeding asshole on the floor, one who flinched back the second Deke grabbed him again, this time to retrieve his phone. Then he handed it to me so I could answer, purposely waiting to see what they would say first,

"Speak to me, Finch, and tell me the fucker is dead, only Gomez is going to shoot someone if he's gotta wait much longer."

"Then if I was you, I would hand the phone over to your boss and then run, cause this fucker isn't as dead as he hoped and neither is my friend... now, I can't say the same for yours, as Finch, well... *he's fucked,*" I told him, making him hiss on the other end,

"Fucking impossible! No fucker would survive that shit!"

"That may be so, but if you wish to speak to me about survival, then you can listen as I play a little game with your friend here, for I do wonder how long he would survive holding his own intestines before dropping them."

"You sick fuck!" he shouted, making me grin.

"Yes, I am, along with *fucking impatient! Now give me Gomez!*" I snarled, a sound that prompted him to act, as I heard him speaking quietly to someone. Relayed information that

18

only took ten seconds and even that was too fucking long for my liking before I heard my enemy come on the other end.

"Who the fuck is this and don't say my worst fucking nightmare or any of that bullshit?!" His high-pitched voice grated against my vessel's spine, while his sinful soul was screaming for my darkness to take him... punish him,

Condemn him.

"I wouldn't waste my time, considering you already know it's true," I replied keeping my cool for now.

"Oh, I do, do I...? Fuck me, can you believe this fucking guy?" he replied, pausing to speak to his people, as it was obvious I was on speaker phone.

"Well, considering you just stole someone who belongs to me, and I am the fucking guy you just dropped a building on and survived... then yeah, I would believe it, Gomez," I replied and again, doing so by keeping my shit together... in other words, *keeping my Darkness in check.*

"Bullshit! I saw the footage and there is no fucking way that asshole survived shit!" I grinned at this as it may have been hard to detect by most, but I recognized the sliver of fear when I heard it.

"Then you clearly don't know as much as you thought you did," I said, purposely stomping on Finch's other knee just so as I could add a backdrop of agony to that subtle threat. He screamed in pain, making Deke chuckle.

"You think I give a shit about a fucking grunt," Gomez snapped.

"Oh, I think he is a little more than a grunt, after all, there can't be that many cops in the bomb squad that you keep on payroll," I said, knowing this information from the brief time I had spent riffling through Finch's head.

"That might be true, but if you think I will fucking trade shit for that fucker then you're not as smart as you are fucking lucky."

"Oh, but you're mistaken, as I wouldn't let him go. No, I just wanted you to hear as I rip out his heart so you know the person you're about to do business with, is fucking serious. After all, we are busy men with shit to do." At this Finch whimpered and started begging for his life. But I twisted my body quickly, slamming my fist down into his chest and doing exactly as I said I would. And well, believe it or not, but the act of removing a person's heart with your bare hands, makes quite a noise. Then after allowing my Darkness to do its job in sending his sinful soul to the only place it needed to be, I turned my attention back to the one I really wanted to kill.

"Fuck! You twisted fuck!" Gomez hissed after first hearing the screams of my victim and then the sound of his rib cage breaking before the squelch of blood and flesh being ruptured to pulp in my fist.

"I'm not twisted, Gomez, what I am, however, is a man who wants what belongs to him returned. You see, you stole something very dear to me and if she is not back in my possession completely unharmed within the next twenty-four hours, well… let's just say, the Wrath of God will look like child's play by the time I am through with you," I told him in my darkest tone.

"I don't take kindly to threats."

"Then how about facts, for if a fucking bomb couldn't kill me, Gomez, what do you think will? I invite you to hold a fucking gun to my head and see what happens when you try and pull the trigger," I snarled dangerously.

"The bitch owes me!" he snapped, making me once again force down my darkness from speaking for me so that I could play my next hand.

"Now, if you want to save me the fucking hassle of getting

bloody, and it's money you want, then I can be reasonable. We are both business men after all," I said, making Deke raise a brow in question.

"Ten mill for the bitch," Gomez offered immediately.

"Done!" I said, making him hiss,

"Damn, but I knew I should have gone higher for the bitch."

"Call her a bitch again and you will get nothing but this dead fucker's head on your doorstep, now where do we make the exchange?" I thundered, making him chuckle.

"That depends on how quick you can pull together ten million dollars," Gomez said, making me snap,

"I am a fuck load richer than you, asshole, so what do you fucking think!?"

"Then that's fucking woopydoo for you and your bitch, then, isn't it?" he replied with a bitter edge I would enjoy hearing change to screaming torture when I ripped out his balls.

"When?!" I snarled.

"Keep Finch's cell on you and wait for the call."

"What's the matter, Gomez, you afraid I am going to turn up at your door and kill you and all your men before the exchange?" I mocked, knowing that of course I fucking would.

"Fuck you, asshole, a fucking army couldn't take down my operation, as you wouldn't make it a fucking step inside this compound before getting your fucking head blown off!" he ranted back, giving me more with his anger than he realized... *giving me exactly what I wanted.*

"Then I suggest not keeping me waiting or we may find out which one of us is bulletproof after all."

"You got fucking balls, I will give you that," he commented, making me sneer down the phone, wishing I had the ability to reach down inside of it and drag his worthless evil soul back through it!

"I also have ten million with your name on it if you hurry the fuck up and give me back what I want!" I reminded him.

"Yeah, yeah, keep your shit together, richy, you will get your girl back."

"I had better, and I warn you, Gomez, she had better get back to me in perfect fucking condition or so help me, I will bury you in that ten million, set it alight and watch as I burn your entire world to the fucking ground with you at the center of it all!" At this I ended the call, throwing the phone to Deke to catch,

"You better take that before I crush the fucking thing!" I snapped, trying to rein in my darkness and ripping off the rest of my torn shirt so I could use it to wipe the blood and bits of flesh that soaked my fist and forearm.

"I take it you didn't miss the part about his compound?" Deke asked as I continued to pull pieces of the once beating heart from in between my fingers.

"If they weren't taking her there before, they will now," I said, gritting my teeth and making Deke point out the obvious, one I had pushed for so it would keep her valuable enough to him to keep alive.

"Yeah, now the piece of shit knows how much she is worth."

I released a sigh.

"And if we can credit him with having any intelligence at all, then the combined thought of ten million and the vivid image I just painted of what would happen should she be hurt, should be enough to keep her from harm until I can get to her."

"And what about this wasted vessel?" Deke asked kicking the very dead Finch.

"Take the head and burn the rest, I am after all..."

"An Angel of my word."

22

CHAPTER 4
OH BROTHER
EDEN

I had to say, from one to ten on the scale of pissed off at being knocked out, I was firmly at a million! Because shortly after I felt the spray of blood hitting my face from the gunshot the guy had received, my mouth was covered from behind. I struggled as much as I could but was soon forced to breathe in some chemical I could only assume was chloroform.

But on that same scale, I had also hit my limit at waking up and finding myself tied to another fucking chair, just like I was now! I also wasn't fortunate enough to be allowed to gradually shake the fog from my drugged mind but instead felt a slap to the face. The heated pain of having a palm hit my cheek was force enough to make me cry out, waking instantly in shock, as the sting bloomed across my cold flesh.

However, I gritted my teeth and didn't give them the satisfaction of crying out a second time as my head whipped one way and then the other, with a back hander this time.

"Wakey, wakey, Miss Teles," I heard from behind me, making it impossible to see as I couldn't turn around. However, what I could see was the heart stopping sight in front of me.

I wasn't the only one strapped to a chair.

My heart thundered in my chest and a small whimper escaped as I tried to make out who it was. His face was covered by a black bag, that despite the color, even I could see was soaked with blood. I knew this as it looked wet, and below it was nothing but blood soaking his shirt as it ran down from his face to his neck.

His now crimson shirt.

But wait. It couldn't be him, it couldn't be Ward.

His shirt had been black.

This was when all the other differences started to filter through, with the most obvious being his size. He was much smaller than Ward, with barely any bulk of muscle to speak of and he was much shorter, despite being slumped in a chair.

"Ah, but I bet you're wondering who our guest is... Heston." It was then that the suited thin man came into view, allowing me now to put his name to his face, and I wished that had been all they had given me. Because after that came the next nightmare, one he forced upon me the second he gripped the blood-soaked bag and ripped it from the man's head. I gasped in horror, not only at the sight of the beating the man had received but mainly, who I instantly recognized.

"Oh no... Jimmy!" I whispered on a pained breath. Because even though he had gotten himself into this mess and dragged me in there with him, he was still a brother to me. One I wished I could hate, but one I knew I never truly would. Because I had too many memories of growing up with him. The things he taught me, the times he protected me against anyone picking on me. He had been there for me...

Once upon a time.

So, despite knowing deep down, that sitting there looking bloody and beaten was not the same Jimmy I had once known, I still cared enough to feel pain at the sight of his agony. The immense swelling in one side of his face, giving only half of him the appearance of still being my brother. A huge gash was gaping across his nose and over his cheekbone, one that looked fractured. And this was just what had been done to his face, which made me dread to think what had been done to his body.

"What have you done... what have you done to my poor brother?"

"Your poor brother, ha now that is fucking laughable!" A nasally voice said before walking from behind me and finally, my enemy came into view, putting a face to the name.

"Felix Gomez." I snarled this time, feeling the venom of hatred uncoil in my belly, desperate to lash out. I watched as he walked toward my brother, making me tense and grit my teeth against the bite of pain that cut into my wrists.

As for the villain in this picture, he was as I imagined him to be. A short man in his fifties, with a receding hair line, podgy red face and more money than most, hence the only real power he held was how much he could pay people to do his bidding. He also dressed like he was stuck in the nineties, with a blue shirt under a cream pinstriped suit. All he seemed to be missing was a Tommy gun and a trilby hat and he would look like a mobster on holiday.

"The one and only, my dear," he replied with a sneer, one made easy with the beady dark eyes and beak-like nose.

"And as for young Jimmy here, well he has caused me quite a few problems, haven't you... *fucker?!* " Gomez said, suddenly grabbing his hair and wrenching his head back, making him whimper. Then he punched him across the face, making me cry out,

"STOP IT!" This just made Gomez start laughing, before he pointed out,

"I thought you would have wanted this little fucker dead more than anyone else, considering he was only too happy to hand his debt over to you." I swallowed hard, making me wince as I could feel the swelling in my cheek. Gomez let his hair go, making Jimmy's head slump forward and a string of blood and drool fell from his lips like some crimson ribbon hanging there before falling into his lap.

"If its money you want then I know how to get it, just let him go," I told him, gritting my teeth to hold back the verbal assault I wanted to add to it. I was also hoping he didn't call my bluff, as no, I had no idea how to get any money.

"Ah yes, I just bet you do, a pretty little thing like you, whoring herself out to some rich bastard with more lives than a fucking cat! Yeah, I just bet you can get me my money..." He paused so he could walk closer to me, having me in his sights to play with next. I knew that when I felt my cheeks being gripped in a meaty hand, making me wince at the pain, seeing as my face was obviously bruised. Then he pulled my face up and grinned when he saw the unshed tears clinging to my eyes.

"A sweet cunt like you... mmm, I can almost smell it, maybe I just take some money owed by making you work my cock for it. Maybe I make Jimmy here watch as I fuck his sister!" Gomez continued to throw filth my way about how he would abuse me sexually, and I swear I was one F word away from throwing up at the thought. By the time it was over, he put his arm around Jimmy like they were best buds, nudging him and saying,

"What'd yah say, Jimbo, should we both have a go at her, huh...? Which end would you chose?" At this I see Jimmy flinch back, and it made me wonder if he too was tasting bile ready to be chased by vomit. Gomez burst out laughing before slapping him on the back as if this was the most fun he'd had in ages.

"Let's put it this way, if I put my fucking gun to your head..." He paused, getting out a large gold gun that looked huge in his podgy hand. Then he pushed the end of the barrel into his cheek making Jimmy start to cry.

"Which would you choose… come on, Jimmy, think about it now… which hole would you use?"

"YOU'RE SICK!" I shouted, making him laugh before he stopped instantly as if struck by an idea.

"I'm sick? I ain't the one who fucked you over first, sweetheart, oh no, that was your flesh and blood right here!" he reminded me, making me turn my head away, sickened by the sight of what he wanted to do to my brother.

"Family is family, regardless of our mistakes," I threw at him with gritted teeth. At this he chuckled and grabbed Jimmy's hair again, he yanked his head back and said,

"Hear that, Jimmy, your big sister still wants to protect you, even after you screwed her over and while you were living it up on the money she gave you, she was sleeping in her fucking car, broke as fuck!" he snarled as if he actually gave a shit, making Jimmy wince at the realization at what my life had turned into since he walked away and left me with all his shit to deal with.

"And you… you still want to protect this fucker?" Gomez asked me in clear disbelief. I swallowed hard and forced my lips to move.

"He's…*He's my brother.*" I answered, making him grin and I swear it was so evil I almost felt it darken his soul that little bit more. It was one that had you knowing those sadistic cogs were turning and the outcome was only going to end one way…

Death.

To prove this, he walked over to me, and this time grabbed me by the hair, pulling my head back, and whispered in my ear from behind,

"Well now, let's test that should we? As I think you will find with this piece of shit here, that loyalty only goes one way." This was when he put the gun to my head from the side,

cupping my face and stroking it like I was pet of his he was holding to ransom. Jimmy jerked up in his ties and tried to struggle.

"Do-don't... ple-please," Jimmy stammered through the pain of split lips and a swollen face.

"Now you have a choice, Jimmy, you can either save yourself or your sister, now which is it to be?"

"You sick bastard..." I snarled, stopping only when his hold on my face tightened painfully.

"Tut, tut, sweetheart, not wise to piss off the man pointing a gun at you... now, which is it to be, I shoot your sister and you walk, or I shoot you and I let this bitch go?" Jimmy jerked again and I watched as his fists clenched at his sides. I knew he didn't want to choose, and I didn't want him to die. So, I took a deep, shuddering breath before telling him with tears rolling down my cheeks,

"*It's...it's okay... it's okay, Jimmy... pick me.*" His eyes widened in shock before he started to shake his head, but my breath caught on a silent cry. Because I knew that right then, one of us was about to say goodbye and this would be the last time we ever saw each other.

One of us would die today.

"*I... can't... I...*" he started to say, tearing his face away, making me say his name,

"Jimmy, look at me... it's okay... just tell him you want to live," I said more firmly this time.

"Aww, how very touching. So, let me get this straight, Eden..."

"Kill me and let my brother go," I interrupted, making him stick his nose into my cheek and growl,

"*How, fucking noble of you.*" Then Gomez straightened up and pointed the gun at Jimmy from where was standing behind me, making me gasp in fear for my brother's life.

"No don't, please…!"

"Shut the fuck up! Now it's your brother's turn, so what is it to be, Jimmy, shoot you or her… time's up, now make your fucking decision, who do I shoot, Jimmy!? WHO DO I FUCKING SHOOT?!" he said, cocking back the hammer and making Jimmy whimper. Then after telling me,

"I'm… I'm sorr-sorry Ed-Edie… *I choose… My Sister,*" he said, making his choice, and I closed my eyes for a second as I let the relief and pain merge into one, knowing that would have been his decision all along. I opened my eyes the second I felt the barrel of the gun against my head, and I watched with tears streaming down my cheeks, as Jimmy, my brother, mouthed one last time that he was sorry, doing so through his own tears.

"I forgive you, Jimmy… I forgive you… now fucking do it!" I shouted, wanting him to get it over with and just hoping that Gomez was going to keep his word and let my brother go. Or my sacrifice would have been in vain.

"As you wish," Gomez said before pulling the trigger and…

Shooting my brother dead.

CHAPTER 5
DEAD OR ALIVE

"NOOOO! YOU FUCKING BASTARD!" I screamed, going crazy after I'd just witnessed him shooting my brother in the head! I screamed out in both fright and utter horror, as I watched his dead body slump forward like some broken mannequin.

"Jimmy! God no... Jesus Christ! You fucking sick bastard, you just killed my brother!" I sobbed, unable to help myself, trying to breathe through the pain at the same time my anger was making my heart pound in my chest. I didn't know what I wanted to do more, tear Gomez's eyes out with my fingernails or fall to the floor and lose myself in my grief.

"Oh please, that piece of shit, I did you a favor, sweetheart," Gomez said with a wave of his hand, like it was nothing. Like I hadn't just lost the only family I had left. My step-dad was in jail and was old enough now that I knew he wouldn't see another free day in his life. But despite his life of crime, I also knew that he had cared about us both... to know his son was dead would crush him.

Actually... *it would kill him.*

I continued to scream at him as the tears blurred my vision, merging my anger and agony and making me fight to get free, welcoming the pain of trying to get out of these cuffs.

"I will fucking kill you!" I snarled feeling the anger build to the point I could almost see the blood of my victim, and I didn't have to wonder what had brought on this killing side of me.

"You can fucking try!" He laughed, making jerk against my cuffs and grit my teeth against the pain I felt as they cut into my raw, damaged skin.

"Let me go and I will show you how well I will fucking try!"

"Oh, so angry, what's wrong doll face, that boyfriend of yours make you feel invincible?" Gomez sniggered.

"You have taken fucking everything from me, you sadistic asshole! So just get on with it and fucking kill me already!" I snarled back, making him suddenly grab my tit and squeeze it hard enough that it brought even more tears to my eyes.

"Or I just tie you up and take whatever the fuck I want before I put a bullet in your brain just like I did with Jimbo over there, make it a joint funeral... I wonder how many would turn up?" I turned my head and snarled up at him,

"Do what the fuck you want, I am already dead inside, fucker!"

"Ha, well that's no fucking fun! I like it when they scream for me," he replied, making me want to vomit all over him and see what fun he would find in that, the sick asshole!

"Yeah, well lucky for you, someone wants your cunt abuse free... damn shame that," he said, making me suck in a quick breath and wonder who. Was it possible that Ward was still alive?!

Could my Hero still be out there!?

"Oh, I see that got your attention, not so quick to want to

die now, eh?" Gomez mocked as he saw the obvious hope start to bloom.

"As for your piece of shit brother, don't waste your tears, sweetheart, as he would have pulled the fucking trigger if I had let him just to save his own skin... fucking karma if you ask me."

"Did you miss the part where I told him to?!" I snapped, making him laugh.

"Fuck, but you got more balls than most of my men, and loyalty that was fucking wasted on Jimmy. Besides, you're too valuable. Because guess what, I got two assholes offering me a fuck load of money for your pretty ass, and only one of them wants you untouched. So, stop turning me on or I may be inclined to go with that offer, despite it being less," he said, groping again at my breast with his fat hand while the other one was rubbing his cock.

I tore my face away and tried to focus on what he had said, making me wonder who the two were that wanted me and more than anything, who was the one who wanted me in one piece?

"Mmm woman, you are making me damn hard... I will tell you what, open that fuckable mouth of yours and suck me off and I will make sure the rest of your stay here is more comfortable," he said, rubbing himself even harder and making me gag.

"I would rather be kept in a fucking sewer, than suck your cock!" I snarled back, making him grab my hair and wretch it back before getting in my face.

"Watch your mouth, girl, or I will knock you out and fuck you anyway... something I may just do yet," he said as if the idea just came to him. He was unzipping his pants, making me start to squirm harder just to get away from him. However, the second he got it out, his phone started to ring, making him swear under his breath,

"What the fuck now!" he snapped looking down at the screen on his phone, and I let out a relieved breath when I saw him tucking his hard cock back inside his pants.

"You got my money, asshole?" he answered, making me tense to the point I stopped breathing.

"Proof of life... Well, you're in luck, as it just so happens that I have her right here with me, as she was keeping me good company, weren't you, darlin'?" I heard the snarl of anger from where I was sitting and again, I allowed myself to hope with every fiber of my being that it was my hero.

"Calm your shit, Warden Za'afiel, yes, I fucking know who you are now!" At this I couldn't help but cry out in relief, something that followed quickly after he placed the phone to my ear.

"Here, lover boy wants to check his cunt is still untouched," Gomez sneered but I ignored this at the thought of something far more important.

"Ward!?" I spoke his name as though I was grasping for a lifeline and dragging it closer to my chest.

"Eden, my Siren, Gods, tell me you are alright," he said, sounding so worried my heart broke.

"Not until you tell me the same about you," I told him, making him sigh,

"Little Carino, it would take a lot more than that to kill me... now answer me, Eden." I swallowed hard, feeling the pain radiating across my face and told him,

"I am fine and am not hurt." At this Gomez grinned down at me as if silently praising me for being a good little captive. He made me sick to my stomach yet again.

"I am coming for you, Eden... do you understand? *I am coming for you."* He said this like a vow to the Gods, making me close my eyes as tears started to fall, making me whisper,

"I will be waiting, hero." At this Gomez laughed and pulled the phone away, making me shout,

"Ward, please be careful!"

"Oh, what a keeper you have here… a real sweet piece," Gomez taunted. I was easily able hear Ward's growling threat on the other end,

"If you fucking touch her, I will rip your fucking throat out!"

"Yeah well, I suggest you meet me with that fucking money you promised, or she won't be one sweet piece anymore. No, she will be in fucking ten of them, all wrapped up and ready for you to go find!" At this I heard Ward roaring in anger, forcing Gomez to pull the phone away so it wouldn't make him deaf. It was done with such force I couldn't help but detect a little sliver of fear show in his wide eyes.

He might have had no idea what was coming for him before.

He did now.

"Just fucking get to C.N. West Chemical Factory before midnight tonight or I start cutting bits off your bitch and I promise, they will be the bits you will fucking miss!" Gomez threatened before hanging up, doing so to what sounded like pure Demonic rage. And for once, I relished the sound because I knew it meant someone's death was on the horizon, and that someone was…

Felix Gomez.

A man who took a moment to seem to come to his senses before he narrowed his gaze, casting his furious gaze on me. Then he back handed me suddenly, making me cry out.

"That is one way to wipe the smug look off your fucking face!" After this he turned suddenly and as he was leaving the room, he barked out his orders,

"Move the bitch into warehouse three, with all the other whores!"

After this, the one I now knew was named Heston, stepped back inside, before motioning his head for the other two men I recognized from before to join him. The one with the ponytail finally relieved me of the pain of having my hands cuffed, and I held back the whimper as they removed them from my bloodied skin. Then I was hauled to my feet with a bruising grip held around the tops of my arms.

The building they started walking me through looked like any typical abandoned building, the only difference was that this one looked to be under construction. Graffitied walls and broken glass were what we started off with but the further we travelled along the empty rooms, the more the building changed as work had been done.

It looked as if this place was intended to be Gomez's next place of business, as he was clearly setting up shop here. But then, as I was walked through the industrial looking space, I felt that horrid pit in my stomach the moment we entered through a long hallway. Door after door made me question just what kind of 'shop' had Gomez set up here when the sickening realization hit me, starting with what he said... *the other whores*.

That's when I knew just what was held behind all those doors.

Girls.

I felt both burning hot anger and rage, alongside the utter sympathy and sorrow for what might become of them. Just knowing what they had most likely already been through was enough to have me snarling,

"You're fucking sick, the lot of you!" Then I was pushed from behind to keep moving, being forced to ignore the sound of girls being sexually abused and no doubt 'buyers' testing out the 'goods' before these girls got sold. Because not only was Felix Gomez in the drug trade, he was also into human trafficking.

All this hit me just when I didn't think I could hate him anymore than I already did. I found out that his soul couldn't get any darker, not even after taking my brother from me! I don't think I had ever experienced a feeling of helplessness quite like I had in this last hour. It had started with Jimmy, my stupid reckless brother who, as soon as I was able, I would start to mourn in what I knew was a bitter way. Because I loved him as much as I had hated him in these last six months. But even then, I had been willing to sacrifice my life to save him and the painful reality was…

That he would have let me.

Because that was the thing about Jimmy, I had fooled myself for so long that the bond I thought we shared had gone both ways. I had fooled myself into believing there was still that protective streak in there toward me. But in the end, when there had been a choice, only one of us had the guts to put the other one before themselves.

Yet despite this, I was glad my last words to him were of forgiveness, just as I was glad his last words to me were words of regret and remorse. That he was sorry for everything. That was what I knew I would hold dear in my heart, and not the bitterness I knew was lurking there in the shadows of my grief just waiting for the moment when I cursed his name. Maybe Gomez was right, maybe his death over mine was karma, or maybe it was just fucking Gomez that needed to die, as he was the root of all this evil!

And speaking of evil, we finally reached the end of the corridor and where the last of the sex cells ended, making me wonder what would happen to the other girls? I would do everything in my power to help. Because I was the lucky one. I was the one with the rich boyfriend willing to pay just to get me back in one piece.

But who did those girls have?

Who would be their hero?

CHAPTER 6

A MAN'S FORTRESS
WARD

"FUCK!" I roared, allowing my other side to break through, pushing past the barriers of my flesh as my darkness swirled angrily around my mortal form. I then released a sigh of pent-up worry and frustration, and a million other new fucking emotions in between, before stepping from the vortex of power that had consumed my body.

"It is as we suspected, she is at the compound," I informed Deke the moment the darkness revealed me from the edge of land that surrounded Gomez's industrial fortress. Because from an outsider looking in, it would have just looked like any other industrialized piece of land that housed factories and warehouses. But it was, in actual fact, the heart of Gomez's operation, and he hadn't been wrong, as he had a small army under his command.

But lucky for me...

He wasn't the only one who had connections.

"I didn't expect anything else from the cowardly little prick," Deke replied with a snort of disgust. *He hated cowards just as much as I did.* But Gomez had, in his anger, let slip about this place, one that admittedly was already on our radar to hit. But timing was everything and unfortunately for me, I was not only outnumbered but also out of my jurisdiction.

"How did she sound?" Deke asked me and as much as I gritted my teeth in response, it was nice to know that he too was worried for her safety.

"She thought I was dead," I told him, making him suck air through his teeth before cursing,

"Fuck."

"She's also scared as fuck, lied when she said she hadn't been hurt and was focusing most of her worry and concern not on her own life but on mine," I said, feeling my knuckles crack as my hands made fists at the thought of them harming her.

"Sounds like the pure soul of a Siren to me."

"And one that will be back in my possession, and fucking soon, or so help the Gods, if anything happens to her, I will…" Deke interrupted me with a hand to my shoulder, keeping me grounded as he told me,

"Don't fucking go there, Ward, we will get her back… speaking of which, let's plan how we make that happen." I looked down at what I could feel was a clenched fist and saw the hellish looking hand that had seeped through without me even knowing it. I was too close to the edge, and my friend knew it. But he also knew it was something that rarely ever happened as I was usually the master of control.

But that was before my Achilles heel.

That was before her.

"Things have changed and so must the plan," I told him. I hoped Gomez had exaggerated the extent of his protection but unfortunately, this was not the case.

"Yeah, 'cause as much as we would have no problem killing every last one of these fuckers between the two of us, our main problem now is keeping your girl safe," Deke replied, being of the same mind set as I. Because as much as I agreed with him on how easy killing these fuckers would be, it didn't change the facts. Which meant the pleasure gained in storming his fucking castle and bathing in the blood of our enemies, was going to have to wait until we could get Eden out of harm's way.

"I would suggest us splitting up and you finding Eden, but I have a feeling Gomez is smart enough that he won't keep her far away and at any given opportunity, he will have a knife to her throat the first second he senses an attack," Deke said, only adding weight to my concerns should we attack now.

"We would have to act quickly," I replied, narrowing my eyes as I took in the layout from where we were situated, looking over a network of what looked like old buildings and new structures. It was clear Gomez was still in the process of rebuilding this site, as Deke discovered he had purchased the abandoned chemical factory six months ago. Since then, he had added a number of new structures, but the main six story building was the one currently getting most of the construction work.

"I hate to say this, Ward but…"

"We are outnumbered," I finished off for him. You didn't spend as much time together as we did and not come to know what the other was thinking. But Deke was right, as all it took was one wrong move and she would end up as a hostage or worse… *a means for revenge.* Because I had no doubt that Gomez was expecting something from me, and I figured that only half of him truly believed I would be showing up with ten million in hand. As for the other half, well… he would be expecting no less than a war. Hence why he was going to stay as close to Eden as possible, because he knew that my girl might be his only leverage should this exchange go south. As for me, I knew it was going to go about as south as it could possibly fucking get…

His world was going to Hell.

As for the money, well, little did he know that ten million meant nothing to me. There was no price I would not pay to get her back safely. However, I also knew that a man like Gomez prided himself on reputation. Which meant that a deal like this would more than taint it, especially if he were to merely let us both walk free after I had handed over the money. Also after I had killed his men, hit one of his plants and destroyed a fuck load of drugs.

No, there was only one way he was going to play this.

He intended to kill us both.

His dark soul told me so.

But then he wasn't the only one out for revenge and well, the simple fact was…

I did it better.

I was reborn into what I am today, as one of Gods' Reapers for the most sinful. As for Gomez, well I would be only too happy to dispose of scum like him, even if this hadn't been personal. But the fact that it was, well, I swear I could practically feel his blood dripping from my hands already. A feeling that made my darkness pulsate beneath my skin, just begging me to release it. The strength of will it took to not just release my wings and swoop in there ready to cause death and chaos was one of the greatest tests I had ever faced.

"Then lucky for us, we have blood thirsty friends in high places," Deke said, morphing that usual easy going demeaner with the rare sight of a sadistic grin.

"That we do," I agreed, turning my back on the temptation to destroy Gomez's world, one that I would soon see reduced to ash and blood at my feet.

Felix Gomez would see his world burn.

This was my vow.

However, to achieve this, I first needed to enlist the help of the man who actually owned New York, as it sure as fuck wasn't Gomez, like he thought. No, that title went to one far more dangerous, and one of the deadliest fuckers around. A Demon I was lucky enough to call friend.

The Enforcer who ruled Northeast America.

Hence why I pulled my phone out of my pocket and dialed the only number I needed, speaking his name the moment the call was answered...

"Kaiden Wrath"

֎

"You're sure about this?" Deke asked as we looked up at a large skyscraper, one I confess that it had been some time since I had been here last.

Kaiden Wrath owned two homes in New York, with this one acting as the heart of his business, both as an Enforcer and as a ruthless tycoon. Hence why I was now standing outside 731 Lexington Avenue, and not at his country mansion in Greenburgh, New York. After my call, he had ensured me that he would gather his team and be on the next flight back here, as I had it on good authority, he was on a secret mission for the King. One that from all accounts, hadn't been as successful as he had hoped.

So, after being forced to wait, I had no choice but to spend my time formulating plans, which included making arrangements for what would happen when I got back my girl. I'd had a meeting with my council and got them up to speed in the video conference. Of course, they had all congratulated me on finding my Siren and in the same breath, had wanted to travel to New York to assist me in taking down Gomez. I confess, I had been half tempted, knowing I would have much preferred to have my own people working with me on this.

But the truth was, New York was not my sector and for me to act without including its sector's ruler, well that would have been going against the rules. Besides, I knew Wrath and his men were more than competent. In fact, they were some of the best at what they did, hence why the King used them and their skills so often.

Which was precisely why I was now staring up at one of the tallest skyscrapers in New York, with its fifty-five-floors that held more than just his private offices and apartments. I walked toward a separate entrance, one I knew not only led up to Wrath's private penthouse suites but his real place of business...

53 Sins.

I walked inside the luxurious lobby of white marble and black glass, and the pretty Demon behind the desk perked up.

"Warden Za'afiel, my Lord Wrath is expecting you." She bowed her head before slipping from her chair. Then with an echoing tap of her high heels on the marble floor, we followed her to the single elevator door. She grinned back at me as she swiped her card at the sensor, and the glossy black doors opened.

This was his nightclub situated on the 53rd floor, yet I chose the floor above, knowing this was where I would find the VIP.

"Gentleman," the Demon offered with a hungry smile, making Deke groan after the doors closed.

"Not your type?" I commented, making him laugh.

"No, I like my balls where they are, and that bitch would have eaten me alive and made earrings of them." I scoffed at this, knowing I would have found humor enough to tease him further, had I not already had a million worries on my mind, all of them starting and ending with the name Eden.

Stepping from the elevator that led up to 53 Sins, I was faced with Wrath's men waiting for me, like I assumed they would. Of course, they knew who I was, as, well… rumors were good for somethings. Meaning those lower on the pecking order took a cautious step back, bowing their heads in respect of another Enforcer.

"Warden Za'afiel, my Lord Wrath is expecting you," Tristan said, a Wendigo Demon who I knew was loyal to the Wrath brothers, as well as being a member of their council. A Wendigo was also known to take on the form of a malevolent spirit, which could possess mortal beings, imitating them for long periods of time. They were also known to invoke feelings of insatiable greed or hunger, feeding from the essence of those that they inflicted. However, there were also those rare types, that fed from the opposite of these feelings, and acts of selfless giving. These were often the strongest of their kind and Tristan was one of them. But this wasn't exactly surprising, not seeing as most Enforcers enlisted the strongest of their kind to sit at a council table, surrounding themselves with power.

Tristan nodded for me to follow him, escorting Deke and I from the lobby and in through the large doors that I knew would lead into the VIP. The first thing to hit me was the essence of humans in the club below that from up here, all seemed to move as one. A heavy club beat pounded through the speakers, creating vibrations that made the whole place seem to hum with power. Lines of strobe lights cut through the shadows of the large open space below, moving in time with the music.

It was an industrial, raw looking space with its iron beams, brushed steel furnishings and black marble floor, one that was barely seen thanks to the mass of bodies below. Now as for the VIP, that was a completely different vibe, and one built more for comfort in mind. Most of the place was filled with large booths adorned in black velvet, each situated on different levels so the club could be easily watched from above. There was a circular glass bar at the center where waitresses travelled to like worker bees buzzing to their hive.

I continued to follow Tristan to the very front of the VIP, that held the biggest space for the powerful beings who owned it all…

The Sons of Wrath.

CHAPTER 7
SONS OF WRATH

I stepped in front of his private space and nodded my respects to the man who had offered to help me…

Kaiden Wrath

He ruled primarily over the Northwest of America, with parts of the Midwest thrown in. America was segmented into four sectors with Wrath working closely with the King of Kings, as Maine was included in that rule. He was also one of the oldest Enforcers, along with myself, due to his heritage. Of course, it helped that Kaiden didn't go anywhere without his brother, Helmer, meaning that Dominic Draven had gained not only one force to help rule here, but two. Hence them being commonly known as…

The Sons of Wrath.

Now, as for the name, this was down to their Demonic heritage, which started with Sathanas, who was the King of Wrath. Sathanas, who fathered this Demonic duo, also happened to be good friends and close ally of Asmodeus, Dominic Draven's father. Another big player in the Hellish world, as the King's father also happened to be the King of Lust, ruling his own realm of Hell. Hence why Kaiden and

Helmer were offered up for the position and lucky for the King of Kings, they had, as they were a force to be reckoned with. But ruling over one of the most powerful city sectors came with a price...

Enemies.

I knew this only so well, and last I checked, Dagon Weaver was an Enforcer still trying to get his hands on New York. Like I said, we all had our own problems with power and those that wanted to steal it from us. But as for right now, I knew that my problem would be in his best interest to solve, for it was quite possible that there was even a Siren out there fated to the big bastard, Wrath.

Because we all had a common goal as Enforcers...

Praying for the Fates to grant us favor enough by gifting us with one of the Eleven Lost Sirens. As for Eden, well she marked the start of the rest being found. So yeah, Wrath would be interested alright, and I had to say, I hoped the hard bastard had it in his fate, for it would be entertaining to watch such a big hard-ass Demon fall to his knees. And well, considering the size of him, he would certainly have a long way to fall.

Kaiden Wrath was six foot five of pure muscle and power. He was bigger than most, being of a size that was closer to the King of Kings, if not slightly bigger. His vessel also looked as if it was a descendant of a Norse God, as he looked like some Viking warrior. He wore his dark hair long, with parts twisted and tied back at the top with the sides shaved close to his skull. His beard was full, but he kept it trimmed into shape, and it was shorter at the sides of his square jaw and tapered down longer at his chin. He also had what I imagined to most was an intimidating stare, with threatening green eyes that would turn black in a heartbeat the second anyone gave his Wrath a reason to come out to play.

His honey-toned skin was also decorated in Demonic

tattoos, some of which were on show as he was dressed ready for the night ahead, just like I was. Black combat trousers, shit kicker boots and a black t-shirt that showed off an array of muscle and tattoos completed the bad ass look. One that told me, he had taken my call seriously.

As for his brother, who was sitting next to him, he was also dressed ready for action, however, that was where the similarities ended. Because Hel was usually the one wearing the suit and was well groomed with what one would call, playboy good looks, and he certainly had the charm to go with it. However, I knew this was a mask he wore, as he was ruthless and cutthroat brutal when he wanted or needed to be. But most of the time, he liked to play it cooler and not as quick tempered as his brother, exchanging cunning intelligence for bulky muscle and size.

This wasn't to say he was lacking by any means, being as big as most other Enforcers, and he had even been known to kick his brother's ass in the ring a time or two. But compared to his brother's immense size, he made up for it in acuteness. The man missed nothing and remembered everything. He was also dark blonde, which was styled longer on the top and shorter at the sides, with no beard to speak of. His perceptive eyes were a startling turquoise-blue color, and he always had a knowing grin playing at his lips, as if amused by most things.

"Ward." Wrath spoke my name in that deep timbre voice of his, at the same time showing me respect with a slight bow of his head. I returned that respect by doing the same.

"Kai," I replied, calling him only few would dare to as the casual use of his name was only ever reserved for those closest to him. But this also let those around him know of the power I held and the position I'd maintained for as long as I had. As let's just say that an Enforcer without loyalty to their King, wasn't an Enforcer for long... nor was he breathing mortal air.

But like I said, the rumors of me had spread throughout the centuries to every far corner of the Earth, hence the respect I usually encountered. And if not, well then, ignorance came with a death wish. Speaking of wishes...

"I wish I could say I was here under better circumstances."

"As do I... come, let us continue this in my office." Wrath stood and at his height, he towered over most people, but it was his immense strength that was showcased in the wide frame of muscles. I was a big man and no slouch in the muscle department myself, but Wrath took it to the next level. His vessel had mirrored his Demonic counterpart, meaning, in short...

Both he and his Demon were fucking big bastards.

As for Helmer's Demon, I happened to know the one thing that could make him lose his tight rein on his Wrath, and that was if anyone ever fucked with his brother.

In fact, I always thought he would have made an excellent Enforcer all on his own, as he was certainly powerful enough. Not that Kaiden would have been eager to see his brother go, as the two were usually inseparable. But even Wrath knew that if the order ever came from the King, then he would have no choice but to let his brother go. As for Hel, well I had no clue how he would have felt about the rise to power, but it was at least worth considering him as a candidate. Especially should the need arise for someone to take the place of an Enforcer who liked to overstep his sector.

Needless to say, they were both as tight as two brothers could be. Hence why they ruled their kingdom as two unbeatable forces. This was most likely the reason they were rarely challenged for their position. The very same reason I myself rarely found it happening. Especially now after centuries of proving my worth as Enforcer and ruler of the largest sector in the mortal realm.

"Come, Za'afiel, you look like you need a drink," Wrath said slapping me on the back, and the strength would have knocked over a lesser man. Thankfully I passed the test and didn't move an inch, something he smirked at before walking past. I granted Deke a knowing look before following the brothers back toward the lobby. Then we rounded the bend and walked up a small staircase that led to his private office situated behind the VIP.

I followed the brothers inside, taking quick note of my surroundings, focusing mainly on the wall of whisky, as he was right, I could do with a fucking drink! As for the rest of the room, this was paneled in a dark wood, matching the large carved desk that was positioned in the middle of the room. One that faced a wall of glass that was an enormous two-way mirror. This was so Wrath could oversee the comings and goings of his club without onlookers peering in. I also knew that he would have had his spell weaver, Teko, summon castings to ensure this privacy. This being another Demon that was a valued member on his council.

Wrath walked straight over to the wall of whisky, his drink of choice, and without asking, poured out four glasses of his finest. I reached for mine and downed it back in one, making Wrath feign insult.

"Fuck, Ward, don't make me start regretting that I gave you the good stuff."

"I've found my Siren," I said, coming right out and saying it, instead of simply hinting at it on the phone this time. His reaction was as expected as his piercing green eyes widened before he whispered,

"Fuck." Then he downed his own drink.

"Eh, come again?" Hel said, putting his own drink down on the nearest side table.

"Are you surprised, as I can assume your reason for being

in England has something to do with orders from the King?" I said, showing my cards because I didn't have time to dick around here.

"Looks like Deke is still good at his job," Wrath said, nodding to my second who was also in dire need of his drink.

"You bet, asshole," Deke replied with a grin and a tilt of his glass.

"That, and I already know of the King's Electus, having witnessed the girl's obvious ability to enamor the King," I added, surprisingly them yet again.

"Then you have seen her?" Hel asked as if intrigued.

"A pretty little blonde who is currently working behind his bar at Afterlife, but it goes without saying that the information doesn't leave this room."

"Don't insult me in my own house, Ward, especially not when you rang me to ask for my help," Wrath snapped, making me grin before nodding my head,

"Force of habit, you understand."

"My asshole brother gets it, don't you, Kai?" Hel responded, making his brother grunt his agreement.

"We already knew of the girl as we were entrusted in seeking out her origins... all the fucking good it did us." Now this did surprise me.

"Ah, so there are some things you don't know?" Wrath commented, making his brother chuckle and push at my second's ego,

"Perhaps Deke is slacking after all," Hel commented with a grin, adding to the jest that would rile up Deke.

"Fuck you, asshole." This time it was said with malice, making me put a hand at his shoulder to center his anger. I then shook my head slightly at him, telling him silently not to rise to it.

"I had assumed he knew all there was to know of her from our last encounter," I replied, making Wrath sigh.

"It seems, the King's Electus is hiding something."

"Then no doubt Ranka will discover the truth as there are few that rival Deke's ability at doing so," I replied, making my point and at the same time, soothing my second's ego.

"We were there to assist Ranka, until we were no longer needed," Hel admitted.

"Then her loss is my gain, for the timing couldn't be better," I added.

Wrath fold his massive arms, making me wonder if his shirt would split at the seams.

"Tell us what you need, and you will have it, my old friend." I nodded my thanks to Wrath before telling them all they needed to know.

"My Siren was only recently discovered, broken down on the side of the road and well... on her way to Afterlife actually," I told them, shocking them once again.

"Fuck me, but that's irony if ever I heard it," Hel commented.

"Try fucking fate, for if I hadn't been there, she would not have lasted long." My words were almost snarled.

"She was harmed?" Wrath practically growled the question, showing his obvious disdain for the thought of any Siren being harmed. But then this wasn't surprising, as we all knew that our fated Sirens were to be protected and well... *worshipped*.

"Yes," I gritted out through my teeth, feeling as if I had failed her the first time by letting her slip through my fingers, despite this being through her own choice. This second time however, she was ripped from them through the condemning choice of others.

"Who would harm her?" Wrath asked in an even more serious tone.

"Does someone know she is a Siren other than yourself, is that why she was taken?" Hel asked right after his brother's question as I had only hinted at her being my Siren on the phone, afraid of whoever else maybe listening at the time. I also told them that she had been taken from me and that I needed their aid to get her back.

"Eden is her name," I said irrationally making Wrath scoff.

"Cute."

"And ironic seeing as Sirens are fated to be an Enforcer's paradise," Hel added, making me snap,

"Yes, well, I fucking want my paradise back, so let's concentrate on how we fucking make that happen!"

"Easy, Ward, we are here to help," Hel warned calmly. However, his brother Kaiden took a more direct approach as he came straight toward me. Then he slapped me on the back through the surrounding deadly mist that had unconsciously started to swirl around me, making it seep back at his touch, for it recognized his power.

"Calm your darkness, my brother in arms, we will get her back to you, this is my vow." I released a sigh and forced that other side of me back into the confines of my mortal flesh, knowing in my anger I had let my control slip.

"Now, do we know who has her?" Wrath asked, walking past me to go and stand in front of the wall of glass that allowed him to see into his club.

I knew once I said the name, he would not grant the VIP his attention for long.

"Felix Gomez." As expected, the second the name was out of my mouth, Wrath turned darkening eyes to me with a predatory grace.

"That fucker took your girl? You're sure on this?" he asked, making me reply,

"Now you insult my intelligence with that question." Wrath shrugged, letting his brother reply,

"Fucking perfect."

"Hardly, given the circumstances!" I snapped.

"Granted, the reasons are unfortunate, but understand, we have wanted an excuse to rid the world of that little shit stain for a while," Hel commented.

"You can say that again," Wrath grumbled in his deep timbre that practically growled his words.

"Then why haven't you?" Deke asked, folding his arms.

"You know the rules and until now, he hasn't broken any by crossing over the line into our world," Hel answered him.

"Until now," I stated firmly.

"Until now." Wrath agreed, this time with a grin that promised nothing but the type of violence his Demon craved.

"I would fucking say so, seeing as the bastard dropped a fucking building on Ward and tried to blow us both to shit," Deke commented dryly.

"That's enough for me, considering this happened in my sector," Wrath said, cracking his knuckles before turning to his brother and saying,

"Get the team ready…

"We have a Siren to save."

CHAPTER 8
PRETTY EYES
EDEN

One night's sleep.

That was all I'd had in the last six months where I had felt safe enough to sleep. One night out of one hundred and seventy-seven, I could I honestly say I had slept well. Yes, I had counted. It had also been the first time I hadn't woken with that sliver of fear of what the day could bring. Ward had given me that and I know for a fact, he had intended for it to be a lot more.

A lot more than just...

One night.

It was a hope I was clinging on to as if it had the power to keep me from taking my last breath. Because Ward was still alive! Of course, the problem with being locked in a room with nothing but your mind to occupy you, was that it gave you time to think. Time to fear. Time to hope.

Time to mourn.

"Jimmy." I uttered his name for the umpteenth time, having the horrifying image of my brother's death play out over and over again, as I couldn't seem to rid myself of the memory. I even knew the pattern the blood spray had made on the wall

behind, making me force the bile down, as I had long ago been reduced to dry heaving. Lucky for me, the room had a toilet next to it, one that had been borderline disgusting, switching swiftly to outright revolting as now it smelled of my vomit no matter how much I had tried to flush it down.

At the very least, it had a door, one that I had been able to close to keep out the smell. But nothing had kept the tears of anguish at bay, because I would alternate between sorrow and guilt. Sorrow for the brother I had lost, doing so for admittedly a lot longer than just today. But as for my guilt, well the moment I heard that Ward was still alive, I shamefully found myself glad that I had survived.

In fact, I had so many emotions rattling around in my head it was giving me mental whiplash. But above all, there was one emotion more prominent than all others...

Worry.

I knew that an asshole like Gomez wouldn't just allow Ward to walk in here and exchange his money for me, something I knew Ward would be willing to do. I kept reminding myself what he had survived already, trying to focus on that, other than all the terrible things Gomez must have planned.

Either way, I kept my eyes glued to that small, barred window and watched as the day came and went, feeling even more nervous as darkness took hold of the room.

One that was bare cinder block walls, with a fold out bed and very little else. It also meant that I nearly jumped out my skin when finally, the door opened. I had already searched the bathroom for any means of a weapon, hoping that there would have been a mirror or something, but there had been nothing, short of ripping the toilet seat off and trying my luck at playing 'hook a duck' with some bad guy.

So, I simply stood, not wanting to give the bastards any satisfaction by acting terrified. Which was why I straightened my back and walked toward the door before they even had to tell me to do so. Because one way or another, this was it, Ward was coming for me, and I wanted to be brave for him.

But strangely enough, this time, as I was led from this building and toward another, it felt different. There were no snide or obscene comments about which holes they wanted to fuck. There wasn't even any need to touch me, they just led the way without so much as a shove or a push. If anything, they seemed...

On edge.

That's when I realized why this was... *They were afraid.* They too knew he was coming and from what I knew of Ward in this short space of time, he wouldn't just be coming for me.

He would be coming for them.

After all, his name didn't mean Vengeance and Fear for nothing. It made me wonder if Gomez knew this too. An answer I soon received the second I heard the men behind me talking in hushed tones,

"I swear Gomez has gone too far this time, this fucker won't stop."

"I heard he took out another warehouse," another one muttered, and I had to do everything in me to suppress the smirk, knowing they were talking about Ward.

"Yeah, well that's nothing, as I heard they found Finch's fucking head on Gomez's doorstep, just like he threatened to do." At this I couldn't help but hold my breath, knowing that Ward's actions were extreme.

"Hence why he's pulled in all his guys for the exchange." I had no idea who Finch was... but unless his doctor's was named Frankenstein then I doubt he would have lived long without his head, so I didn't really care. But this wasn't the part that most concerned me, which just proved how much I had changed considering I was accepting the fact my boyfriend decapitated someone was well, meh. No, what worried me was just how many men did Gomez have? Because I knew Ward was clearly a supernatural badass, but he was only one man and from the sounds of it, Gomez had a freaking army!

"You know the drill, now sit your ass in the fucking chair," I was told by Heston, who I saw first when we entered the room. We had walked a different route this time and crossed over a large courtyard that was surrounded by different buildings in different states of construction. The one we headed to looked like nothing had been done to it at all and was being used as a place of storage for heavy machinery and building materials.

As for the room they brought me into, it was a large space with tall ceilings that had dirty glass windows above. It also looked as if it had long ago been gutted down to its bare walls. There were parts patched with lighter paint, as if shelving used to be fixed there once upon a time. However, now all it held was a single chair in the middle and the gangster thug who wanted me to sit in it.

I did as I was told because really, what was the point of trying to fight it, as getting myself killed before my Hero turned up was not the outcome we were hoping for. However, this didn't mean I couldn't help snapping,

"Again... really?" This was in response to baldy coming toward me with rope and a fucking grin on his face I wanted to scrub off with a dirty toilet brush! Of course, my complaints meant nothing but giving him the satisfaction of tightening them to the point I couldn't help but whimper in pain. Then the bastard winked at me, making me exchange that imaginary toilet brush for a semi used wax strip that had come from some back, sack and crack appointment!

Good one, Edie.

I mentally patted myself on the back for that one, needing

something to keep me from completely freaking out and getting hysterical.

"He's here… get ready," Heston said, making me tense the second I heard guns being cocked. I frowned at the sound of more men entering through one of only two doors. However, I ignored the one at my back and focused instead on the one I faced, which was the one I knew Ward would be walking through any second now. I looked around, trying to see where all the noise had come from as there was only a handful of men in the room with me, all at the ready.

But that sound, had it echoed?

Thoughts disappeared the second I saw him enter through the door ahead and his eyes didn't take even a second to scan the room. No, *they just went straight to me.* As for my own, I felt tears instantly appear at just the sight of him. As if I hadn't truly believed he was alive until that very moment, only clinging on to hope that it was true. Like a dream, I purposely pulled on my restraints, needing the sting of pain to anchor me to the moment, making me realize that it was real.

I wasn't dreaming.

My Hero was really here.

But I wasn't the only one who looked relieved as even he closed his eyes a moment as if silently thanking his Gods. He looked dressed for action, wearing black army trousers, thick boots and a black tee under a black combat jacket. He also carried with him a large duffle bag that I assumed held a shit load of cash.

"Which one of you dogs is going to go fetch your master and tell him to come collect his money?" Ward said with a level of authority that made me shiver at the power of it.

"Gomez is on his way," Heston replied, obviously being the one put in charge of this exchange.

"Yeah, sure he is," Ward replied dryly before taking a step

toward me, not stopping when guns were raised pointing at him.

"Payment!" Ward snarled and continued to walk straight toward me, tossing the bag off to one side next to one of the gunmen and totally ignoring the threat. No, instead he stepped right to the side of me and gently took hold of my chin so he could assess my face.

"Ward." His name came out like a whispered prayer, and it was a sound that affected him.

"My Siren, did they hurt you?" he asked with the deadly threat of that question thickening the air like some dark promise. I swallowed hard and thought it best not to make him worry, so simply shook my head to tell him no. At this his eyes narrowed slightly but then the back of his hand stroked featherlight down my bruised cheek where I had been hit the hardest.

"Didn't I tell you never to lie to me," he told me softly, making me suck in a breath. One that was quickly followed by a louder gasp the second the room suddenly started to fill with no less than twenty guys with guns, telling me now exactly what that noise had been.

A small army getting ready.

"Dumb fucker actually brought the money... but wait, what's this underneath!?" Baldy said, making me flinch before I was scowling at the bastard.

"Eyes on me, sweetheart." Ward's gentle command worked, making me look back up at him. But the second he saw the worry in my eyes, I felt the tears start to fall at the thought of what all those bullets could do to him.

"Please, Ward... run while you still can." At this he leaned down and whispered,

"I am right where I need to be, My Little Carino." Then he straightened as if we weren't surrounded by a small army.

"Hey boss you need to…"

"Shut the fuck up, Ricky!" Heston snapped as the bald guy tried to explain what it was he was looking at in the bottom of the bag, making me wonder what Ward had brought with him.

"Now as for you, Gomez sends his regards, Asshole," Heston said with a smirk, making me hold my breath, too afraid to let it go. But that's when the strangest thing happened, as Ward just grinned down at me.

"I bet he does," he replied as they started to get into position to kill us both, making me realize that this was only ever meant to be an execution. Yet one look at Ward, and that was when I also realized the truth of what this was, being the very thing they still didn't understand,

It was no longer our execution.

No… *it was theirs.*

I knew that now. I saw it the second Ward's eyes blackened as his Darkness started to seep through his handsome face. Then, with a tender touch to my face, stroking a thumb under my eye, he told me,

"Now, it's time to close those pretty eyes for me."

"Why?" I whispered even though I already knew.

I knew.

"Because it's time to show them who I really am… it's time…" he paused long enough to allow his Darkness to fully appear and a frightening breath later, he told them all…

"…For sinful souls to pay."

CHAPTER 9
WHEN DARKNESS COMES
OUT TO PLAY

T he moment he said this, all Hell broke loose, *literally*.
It started when Ward threw his hands up quickly, creating a stream of darkness to expand outwards from the lower part of his body. The smoky branches then flew up and hit each of the men just at the same time they opened fire. This meant that each bullet ended up in the ceiling as all their guns were knocked upwards so violently, it looked difficult for them to hold onto, being jerked forward a step with the force.

I knew at this point I should have closed my eyes, but I found myself without the ability to do so. My need to check that Ward stayed alive far outweighed whatever terror I might experience. Of course, that was until the true horror really started.

One that was signaled by the first scream of pure dread, that ended with a gargled sound of an agonizing death. This was after I witnessed Ward literally rip a guy's throat out before moving quickly onto his next victim. It was as incredible as it was frightening, watching as the shadow of his mortal form followed in the footsteps of his Darkness. Then, it latched back onto him, morphing his once handsome face and incredible body into the same Demonic figure I had seen that day outside of Afterlife.

Christ, but it didn't even look as if he was barely trying to kill these guys, it was just happening. Doing so with such ease it had me shaking in fear, despite knowing he would never turn such a brutal side toward me. But then this was why he had wanted me to close my eyes. He hadn't wanted me to witness this side of him. Something he realized the second a frightened gasp escaped me a heartbeat after he had just given someone his last. This he had done by punching his fist through someone's chest cavity with a Demonic covered hand.

Even through the chaos of screams, the erratic gun shots were never aimed at anything other than the ceiling. As after one of the men tried to reach me to use me as a human shield, Ward's Darkness had shot out like some extended limb of a Demonic sea creature. A long tentacle that speared him in the chest and pinned him against the wall, making me scream this time.

Then, after he retracted this, making the dead man drop to the floor, the tentacle was used as an extension of his arm, as he gripped the chair, I was sitting in. Then I cried out in shock as he yanked it toward the side of the room that was clear, making the back of it hit the wall. I shook from side to side until being pushed upright by his Darkness and this time, I didn't flinch as it touched me.

But then through the fog of his Darkness Ward stepped toward me and I was suddenly transported back to that day. The living essence that swirled around his form as though it lived and breathed each day with him. The way it created a veil of a hood that, like that day, cast his handsome face in shadow. As for his body, it was once again bigger, with combat clothing now replaced by black plated armor that seemed to be alive as it was constantly moving. It looked made from stone one moment and then smoke the next, yet the two spiked horns that rose straight up from where his neck met his shoulders never changed. And just like he had that day, he looked like some Hellish warrior on the warpath.

A warrior that continued to approach me, and despite how frightening he looked, he still managed to grant me a soft tender look, tilting his head a little. Then he lowered down to one knee as if to make himself appear less fearsome, now putting him only a foot taller than my head height. Because in this other form he always seemed so much larger, towering over me even more than he usually did.

He reached out slowly, and this time it was the smooth back of a talon that caressed my face, making me wonder how it was possible for such a killing machine to be so gentle and tender.

"You should have closed your eyes, Siren," his gravelly voice said, making me wonder if he wasn't half Demon after all, as he most definitely gave the impression of one.

"But then who would have your back?" I told him quietly, making him grin and despite how evil it looked, I knew differently. But then as if this moment between us was fated, the second I saw one of the men standing and point their gun at him, I screamed,

"BEHIND YOU!" He closed his eyes and then a hand shot up just as the gun had been fired. Unbelievably he caught the bullet mid-air. I cried out in utter shock and had my hands been free, I would have covered my mouth.

He was incredible!

But then I watched as his anger morphed his features to something even more Demonic and he stood, at the same time making his hands extend out behind him. This caused all his darkness to blow backward, like a sandstorm sweeping across the desert. It was like a wall of death as it hit into each of the men, despite most of them being dead. I then cried out in horror as I saw it strip each body of their life, starting with skin, then flesh and then finally reducing each of them to nothing but bone. It was as if some flesh-eating particles were in the air, cursing the living until it swept up the bones, crushing them to dust in Ward's vortex of destruction.

After this came the calm after his storm, as it started to float gently to the floor, casting the dusty remains toward the corners of the room like grey sand.

"Eden, take slow, deep breaths for me," he said, drawing my eyes back to him now looming over me. It was only now that I realized I was panting and I raised my watery gaze up to his dark one. Then he placed a hand to the back of the wall behind me, and leaned in close, telling me again in a sterner tone,

"Breathe for me." I swallowed hard through labored breaths and nodded, unable to speak. He leaned to the side a little and with a bit of a tug, I felt him rip through the rope with the ease of his talons. After I was free, I stood quickly, making the chair knock sideways. He seemed surprised by my quick actions and gave me space, taking a few steps back.

"Don't fear me, Eden," he said in a tense tone, but I'd had enough.

Had enough of waiting.

Which was why I practically ran into his arms, taking him off guard for only a moment as I jumped into him. Thankfully he caught me in time, as he seemed astonished. Then I reached up and gripped his horn and used this to yank him to me, growling my own words,

"I would never fear My Hero." Then I kissed him, no longer caring which side of him I got to claim, as long as he started to claim me back. Something that took him no time at all to do, starting with the way he growled in my mouth. I shuddered against him at the animalistic sound, something that

only managed to turn me on even more. Just like when I felt him gripping me by my ass, hoisting me further up him so he could consume me in what was now his own dominating kiss.

I vaguely felt myself being walked backward but this was only confirmed when I felt the wall hit my back. This made it easier for him to pin me in place, both with his hips as my legs were wrapped around his waist, and the feel of his solid armor only made it more dangerously erotic. As though I was about to be fucked by some dark, Hellish knight that had the power to destroy a room but was as gentle with me as if I had been made of glass. The two extremes were only adding to the pleasure and just from rubbing myself against the hard outline of his cock had me coming far quicker than I could have ever imagined.

I threw my head back and screamed at the ceiling, seeing the swirling obscurity above me, making me realize he had cocooned us in his Darkness. I continued to use him, rocking against him as I rode out the rest of my orgasm, making him growl in response. A sound that would have once scared me, but this time it only drove my passion for this man, for this beast, higher.

"Perfect... fucking perfect for us," he rumbled before tucking my face into his neck so he could lean his horns against the wall above my head. I couldn't help but hold onto him tighter at that, loving that he spoke of both him and the other dark side of him.

Then I felt him start to change as my body still clung to him, feeling the harshness of his amour reduce to the man I first watched walk in here to save me. After that, he wrapped his arms around me and held me to him as if I meant everything in the world to this man.

As if I was always Fated to be his.

CHAPTER 10
LAWS OF ENFORCEMENT
WARD

Gods be thanked.

She was safe.

My Siren was safe. Safe and finally back in my arms. Fuck, but I had to be careful not to crush her to me, forcing myself to be as gentle with her as it was physically possible in this form. I knew she had been frightened of that side of me, as I had felt it...

Shamefully, I had even fed from it.

Just as I had from the rest of the men that I had eradicated. It was why I hadn't just walked in there and unleashed that deadly wave I was capable of. As for that, I had first needed to drink my fill of fear. But then, the second some fucker decided to shoot me instead of doing the sane thing and making a run for it, I had lost my supernatural shit. Because she once again had my back and the knowledge pierced my heart like that bullet had intended.

Had I not been on my knees already, then I would have fell to them and worshipped at her feet. She was such a gift! One I only ever wanted to protect and love until the end of days and beyond. Hence why I forced my darkness back so I could take her in my arms, picking her up and cradling her slight form to my chest.

Ideally, I had wanted her to close her eyes and protect her against what horrors I was truly capable of. But I was starting to understand now that Eden was far stronger than that. I knew this the moment I released her and instead of running in fear, an action I wouldn't have blamed her for...

She ran toward me.

Fuck me, but I had never in all my lives ever felt the kind of happiness I did in that moment. Because for the first time since my very existence on this mortal world began...

Punishment from the Gods had never felt so fucking sweet.

Had never felt so right.

And for the first fucking time in too many Gods be damned years to count, falling from the Gods good graces had never felt so significant, so worth it... *so fucking perfect.*

That was why this had been the first thing I said to her after she finished shuddering in my arms, finding her release at the most unlikely of times.

In the arms of a condemned yet now blessed Angel.

However, she had no idea the depth of what these words had meant, for in that moment I wouldn't have had the knowledge or even the strength to put it into words. So, I didn't try, I just let her feel, hoping it was enough. Then I carried her out of this personal hell of mine, all too ready to eradicate it both from memory and from Gomez's world.

Of course, I knew that cowardly little fuck wouldn't be anywhere near the exchange. No, that would have been too easy. Hence why my first goal had been to get Eden out of there and safe before I had chance to take care of business. Had chance to take care of Gomez and my revenge.

Once and for all.

And speaking of revenge, I heard them long before Eden

did, not surprised that by the time I walked out of the warehouse with her still in my arms, we were once again surrounded. The front of the older building was off to the side and further from the gates that, unsurprisingly, had been heavily guarded. We had scoped out every inch of this place we could, yet none of us were convinced that this had all been Gomez's men. It would have been too easy, which was why Helmer wasn't the only one to believe there must have been underground bunkers on site, as I had expressed the same concern.

And it looked as if we had been right, as here they were, now surrounding us when we were only thirty feet from the building I had just saved her from.

"Oh shit," she muttered the second she saw the army of guns all pointed at us from the tactical team of mercenaries I already knew Gomez had hired. Because using his own men had only been a smokescreen to hide the real plan. As now I wasn't facing handguns, but automatic weapons. A quick glance behind and I soon realized this wasn't just from the front, but from all around. This meant that there must have been some hidden bunker somewhere with direct access to this building.

"Ward, if we don't survive this, I want you to know that I love you." At this I felt warmth flood my veins and told her,

"My Love, we aren't going anywhere." She frowned in question, making me whisper down at her,

"He isn't the only one who brought back up."

"Gomez told me to tell you, this is what happens when someone fucks with him," a man said. He was standing at the center of the twenty or so men he had under his command, and seeing as he was older than the rest, I would say he was retired military. He also had that air of commanding authority about him, which he most likely never got used to not having when he was forced to become a civilian again. He still kept the same buzz cut and stood as though he was still a sergeant. Well, it was time I gave him a different type of retirement, one of a more permanent kind.

Which was why, as soon as this threat had been said, I started laughing, making Eden look up at me as if I had gone crazy. Then I gave my own signal, and Wrath's team seeped out of the shadows totally unseen, as was the plan all along. Then, just as his men were beginning to open fire, I surrounded the both of us with my wings, pulling Finch's detonator from my pocket and pressing the button, making the building behind us blow, killing far more than Finch had ever anticipated it ever would.

"AHHH!" Eden screamed, gripping me tightly as I opened my wings in time to see Wrath in his other form, using his powers to wipe out most of the mercenaries in one blow. His huge Demon would no doubt be considered more as a monster to mortals witnessing this sight before their death. His skin had been replaced by what looked like cooled lava, with the charred spikes of his many horns already burst from his mortal shell. A part of him that was effective enough when he shoulder barged a man to the side of the wall, pinning him there after impaling him.

The rest of his men continued to fight, including Hel, who chose not to change like his furious brother. No, instead, he continued to take out these guys with stealth and skill, moving with ease and making his killing look effortless.

As for myself, I ignored the flames behind me, and hoped that my wings drowned out the sounds of men being burned alive for Eden's sake. I then watched those that were thrown into buildings like they had been catapulted by a machine and not by a being the size of Hel, as he certainly seemed to be enjoying bending their guns in half before tossing them aside. I was just glad Eden's hearing wasn't as acute as mine, as I could hear the bones cracking from here.

But then I saw Wrath about to kill the commander of this team and I told him in a deadly tone,

"That one is mine!" Wrath just shrugged his large, horned shoulders and punched him once with enough force to make most of his face split but wasn't enough to kill him. He then dropped the howling man to the floor as I continued toward the van that was parked close enough. It was one that Deke had driven inside the compound the moment I made my signal for Wrath's forces to move in, as per my instructions.

Speaking of which, my second saw me coming and quickly opened the side door, allowing me to lower my girl inside.

"I won't be long," I told her, but she grabbed my hand quickly, not letting me go.

"Do you... do you have to?" she asked in a tone that nearly broke my fucking heart. Then she looked down as if ashamed, something I didn't like so much and therefore wouldn't tolerate. Which is why I took possession of her chin in my gentle grasp, and raised her head up so she could grant me her beautiful, watery eyes. They were like glass windows to what I knew in that moment was a fragile soul. Which was why I wiped away the few tears that managed to escape and asked her,

"I just need you to be brave for me a little longer... do you think you can do that, Little Carino?" At this she swallowed hard and nodded her head, making me remind her gently,

"Words little one, I will always want your words." Again, she squirmed under my intense gaze before telling me quietly,

"I will be brave for you, Ward." I let these words soothe my soul and before I could think a second longer, I hooked my palm behind her neck and pulled her in for a hug, cradling her head to my chest. I kissed her hair before releasing her enough so she could look up at me and I swear, I nearly came undone.

So, fucking sweet.

However, I don't tell her this. No, what I did do was put my forehead to hers and tell her fervently,

"I am so fucking proud of you." Then I kissed her after tipping her head back for my lips, needing to force myself to leave her loving warmth that heated my body like no other.

"This won't take long." She nodded at this and when I raised a brow in silent chastisement, she smirked and gave me what I wanted.

"I will be here waiting for you, Hero." I winked at her and finally forced myself to let her go. Then I walked toward my waiting victim. I also granted Deke a look, telling him without words to prevent Eden from seeing what came next. He got the message, and as soon as she was out of the line of sight, I continued with my mission. One that started by putting my foot on his throat and applying enough pressure to get his attention. He was barely recognizable as the man who had arrived here with the sole purpose of killing me and my Siren. A fact that had signed his death warrant the moment he was foolish enough to take this fucking job, long before he met me.

Foolish mortals.

"Where is Gomez and I will make this death quick?" I said, at least giving him that. He spit up the blood he had no choice to swallow, thanks to one punch from Wrath that broke most of his face. I would be lucky if the fucker could even still talk. Something that was looking less likely if all the blood he was spitting up was anything to go by. That crimson grin was one of pain not humor.

"Point to a fucking building then, as I know he is still here," I growled down at him, and just to speed things up, I let him see my Darkness, using it to reach out past my human face as if it was ready to take a bite out of him. He looked beyond fucking terrified and quickly used a shaky hand to point toward another building, the one that was the tallest. It was also the one that was having the most work done on it, as all around the outside of it looked like a construction site. It looked like Gomez was spending a shit load of money on this place, and I couldn't fucking wait for him to watch as I burned the whole fucking lot to the ground just before he died!

I snarled up at it and nodded so Wrath and his men knew where we were to focus our attention next.

"Gomez is mine," I snarled, making Wrath laugh like a sadistic fucker and motioned for his men to gather round. As for me, I looked down at my victim and just before I stomped down on his throat and stepped over his useless body, I told him the last thing he would ever hear before I sent his soul to Hell.

A warning for him to take down there with him.

"And this is what happens when you…"

"…Fuck with an Enforcer."

CHAPTER II
ALL GUNS BLAZING
EDEN

"I wouldn't look if I were you," Deke warned, making me look up to see him standing guard.

"Would it make him someone different if I didn't?" I asked, causing him to first raise a brow at me, as he was clearly surprised by my question.

"No, it wouldn't." I looked back at Ward as he casually stepped over his latest victim and then told his friend,

"Then why would I look away when it's both sides of him who I have allowed myself to fall in love with?" At this I saw the man in question quickly turn to look at me, along with the rest of the men that were clearly on our side.

"Erm… they all just heard that, didn't they?" Deke chuckled at this as Ward received a hand slapped to his back from the biggest man of the lot, before he started stalking toward me.

"What do you think?" Deke replied with a cocky whisper, then he winked at me before stepping aside as Ward approached. Then, without even a word, he took my face in both hands and claimed me in a kiss before all words I might have said were spoken. No, in fact, the only sound I made was

the moan that slipped free when he kissed his way down to my neck and growled into my flesh.

"Can't fucking wait to get you home," he snarled, making me shiver and I swear, I was half tempted to try grinding myself against him again in hopes of finding my next release. But then I think some people may notice me trying to dry ride myself on his big dick again.

Ward suddenly froze, tensing his muscles as soon as the sexual thought painted the image. I would have questioned why but then the second I heard booming laughter, I whipped my head toward a team of tactical looking men, with half of them grinning at me and the other half trying to look anywhere but at us. Even the biggest one, who was now walking away from the others, was shaking his head as if he had just heard something hilarious. That's when I turned my mortified gaze back to Ward, who was smirking down at me as though he just couldn't help it.

"Oh God... You're not the only one who can read minds, are you?" At this he tried to contain his own laughter, but nothing could contain the smirk that was fighting to break out into a full-blown grin. He then shook his head, telling me no, and I let my head fall, faceplanting into his chest, muffling my moan,

"Damn my horny brain." This time he cupped the back of my head and chuckled.

"If the order came from the Gods themselves it would be of no matter, for no such power could force me to damn such a thing I love." At this I looked up at him and said,

"Don't make me drag you inside this van, Hero." At this he smirked and whispered his reply, only inches away.

"Don't make me let you." Then he pretended to nip at my lips with a playful growl.

"Please tell me we are leaving soon," I groaned, making

him chuckle as he knew now why I wanted to get him alone so bad... hell, now everyone did!

"You are, and I will follow shortly." At this my grip tightened onto his jacket and held him to me.

"No, I am not going without you!" I told him firmly, making him sigh out my name,

"Eden..."

"No, Ward, it's not happening... it's not..." I tried again, only getting so far until he interrupted me.

"Ssshh now, calm for me. You will be safe, I give you my word. My friends over there are going to have their men take you back to their base and..." This was when I pulled myself up to get in his face and said more sternly,

"I. Am. Not. Leaving. You." His sigh this time was heavier as he saw my determination, knowing this was another fight he would have on his hands.

"Besides, I want to make sure that the other girls are safe and..."

"What other girls?" Ward interrupted, making me gasp.

"Wait, you don't know?" His frown only backed up this statement.

"When I was brought here, I was taken from one place to the next and along one corridor there were girls held in what looked like cells." At this he hardened his jaw and a second later, he growled the order,

"Stay here." I reached for him and told him shamefully,

"Ward, it sounded like... *like they were being sexually abused."* At this he closed his eyes for a few seconds and then pulled me close, holding me because he knew I needed it. *We needed it.* Something I discovered when he pulled back and after running the backs of his fingers down my bruised cheek, he asked,

"Other than this... *tell me they didn't touch you?"* The

second he said it, I could help it, my mind went back to Gomez and how he grabbed my breast in a bruising hold, getting out his cock ready to try and force me to suck it. But I knew my mistake the second I heard the dangerous sound and this time, it was one I had foolishly caused.

"Ward, I…"

"RWAAARRR!" Ward thundered, making me jump a mile and I was forced to hold my hands over my ears.

"That fucker is GOING TO DIE!" He roared this last part and as I reached out to try and hold onto him, I knew it was useless as he ripped himself from my feeble hold. But I quickly left the van and started following him. He erupted into his other form with his wings bursting free and causing me to falter in my step. However, I steeled my nerve and ran after him.

"Damn it, Ward!" I shouted, and the scene quickly got the notice of the men all standing around who I assumed was their leader, a man I had barely noticed before. They all turned their heads our way, but I didn't care, running for him in earnest. Then I reached for him, making him snarl down at me as if it was an instinct. However, I wouldn't be bullied and knowing that he wouldn't hurt me, I pushed his chest and told him,

"Don't you dare growl at me, you big ape!" At this he jerked back, as if his shock had forced this reaction from him. Some sniggers were heard behind me and he snarled at them, making them shut up pretty quickly. But he wasn't the only one, as I also shot them a scathing look over my shoulder.

"Oi, don't pretend you never saw a pissed off girlfriend before!" I snapped at them, before turning my attention back to Ward, poking him in the amor and hurting my finger… as fuck me, it was hard. He turned back to me just as I was mouthing a silent,

'Oww'

"I like this chick," one of the other men muttered, and it had to be said he was gorgeous and had my own totally sexy scary ass boyfriend not already been so utterly ingrained in my heart, then I might have taken more notice. But as it stood, Ward growled at him, making the man wink, totally unafraid. Telling me he was either utterly fearless, suicidal, stupid, or another mega badass who was just as powerful. And with that cunning glint to his startling blue eyes, I was going to bet my shitty car on it being the last.

"Great, that's nice, but when he's not being an irrational ass, I'm his," I told the handsome man, making Ward grab me to him as if trying to prove a point by tugging me to the side of his armor that was definitely less stabby and deadly.

"You are always mine, woman!" he snarled down at me as I rolled my eyes.

"You will pay for that one later, my little Siren," he warned, making me sigh.

"Fabulous, just what I need after my stay at Mobville, a bad girl spanking." At this he finally allowed himself to grin, but I pressed on.

"Look, I get it, you want to kill the guy, and that's great… Hell, I will pass you the pointy shit to do that… erm… not that you need it," I said, after first pressing a fingertip to his spiked armor and pricking myself accidently, well, kind of on purpose. But then, before I could put it in my mouth to clean the blood from my finger, he had shackled my wrist in his Demonic looking hand and was bringing it to his own mouth to suck on.

"You were saying, Little Carino?" he asked, giving my finger one last lick.

"I just don't want you acting rash and doing what he would want you to do. Gomez might be head of the douchebag parade but he's still in charge of his fucked up little world for a reason. He certainly didn't get there with charm and good looks, baby." His dark gaze softened hearing this, and if I could pinpoint the part he liked most, then I had a feeling it was the endearment at the end.

"The girl is right, Ward, the other buildings have been too quiet during this whole time, as we all expected more than what we have encountered so far," the dark blonde-haired man said, making Ward ask,

"Where is your brother, Hel?"

Wow, okay, so his name was Hel... not the most subtle name for a Demon surely. He granted me a grin at this thought, making me inwardly cringe as I kept forgetting my inner thoughts were basically on speaker phone.

"He agreed with me that things seemed off, so he took it upon himself to check out the other warehouses, he should be back any..." Hel never got to finish this sentence as suddenly, explosions erupted all around us, making me scream. But I also noticed that despite having Ward's arms around me, protecting me, all the men closest to us did the same. One man even went as far as throwing up some kind of spell to mask the damage so we were protected. I swear he looked like a wizard when he threw up a silver shimmering shield, and I watched with wide-eyes and mouth agape when the flames hit it. The flames turned to black smoke the second they touched the shield-like thing, as if it was a wall of water dousing the flames.

But this was all I saw as I was suddenly picked up and swiftly found myself sheltered, firstly by Ward's wings and then by the van I was put in. This happened in seconds and literally made my head spin, to the point that I was still mentally asking myself what had happened, something Ward answered.

"We are under attack. Deke, take her back into the city and get her to Lexington." I grabbed him and pleaded with him,

"Come back to me, Ward! Please be careful and get back to me!" He placed his forehead to mine and told me ardently,

"I give you my word, the Gods wouldn't be able to stop me."

"And the girls?" I asked, making him look me in the eyes as he gave me his vow.

"We will save them all," he replied, before pulling away and nodding to Deke. But this was when his plans of getting me out of there started to go to shit. Because the ambush was now coming from both sides, and I was forced to watch as the next few seconds played out in slow motion.

I screamed as Deke saved Ward by pushing him out of the way of what looked like a grenade, one Deke deflected with a burst of his blinding white wings that quickly turned into a solid black wall that exploded themselves. The result of this blew the grenade back with the force of it, making it fly back toward the enemy, taking out a truck they had being using to drive closer.

Then he turned back to the van and slammed the door closed, making me run toward the windows at the back so I could see what was happening. Deke tried to get to me, but suddenly he was being forced to fight, knocking the wave of soldiers that all came shooting, using some sort of invisible power to deflect the bullets from the van.

"I will deal with them, just get her out of here!" Ward thundered, before I watched his form fly over to the group, landing hard enough that it knocked them all back. But then, just as Deke was making his way to me, I saw the snipers on the rooftops, making me scream as the first shot pierced through the metal doors, just missing me. Deke saw this and snarled their way before unleashing his own invisible power and pushing it like a vortex toward the roof. A force I only just managed to make out as it warped and twisted the world around it.

But then I heard the driver's side door open and slam shut, making me turn in horror toward a man in black fatigues.

"I'm getting you out of here," the man said, making me sigh in relief as for a moment I had thought he was one of the bad guys. Then he started driving, swerving around who I could now see was the rest of Hel's team, fighting with what looked like impossible odds as there were now hundreds of soldiers attacking them. But when one man had the power to take out five at a time, I knew it wouldn't be long before we were winning again.

I glanced back to see Deke watching the van speeding away and just before he could get to me, he was shot down to his knees as he had that many bullets firing at him. I couldn't stop myself from crying out at the horrific sight.

"NO!" I screamed, making the driver look back at me and when he did, that was when I noticed he wasn't dressed like Hel's men.

He was however dressed like...

One of the bad guys.

CHAPTER 12
THE WRATH OF BEING TAKEN

I tried not to react, pretending I didn't know that he was one of the bad guys. No, instead I simply played along, knowing he would just use that gun strapped to his thigh if he wanted to force me into doing whatever they had planned.

"We need to get the fuck out of here!" I shouted like the panicked girl I was, purposely not keeping this part in, as it would make it more believable.

"We know a place," he said, driving closer to the gates and passing the large courtyard I remembered crossing.

"Is it further outside the city like Ward said?" I asked, just making sure that I most definitely did have my suspicions right about the guy. Then I scanned the van and pretended to fall as soon as I saw something that I could use. Not my first choice, granted, but it was going to have to do.

"Yeah, that's the plan," he agreed, and I swear this guy wasn't even trying. So, I stumbled a step toward the front and the moment I was close enough, I put the screwdriver to the back of his neck and collared the front, holding both tight enough so he would know I meant it.

"Wrong answer, asshole," I told him, admittedly feeling like a badass for the first time in my life.

"You don't want to do…" His threat was suddenly cut off with a loud pop before the sound of crunching metal followed.

"Fuck!" the driver shouted, and suddenly the van seemed to lose its path and slammed into something, throwing me forward enough that the screwdriver in my hand stabbed up inside his brain, making me cry out in horror.

"Oh my god, oh my god! I just killed a… oh wait, phew it wasn't me," I said the second I saw a bullet hole in his chest, knowing this was why he lost control… speaking of which…

"Oh fuck!" I shouted, as the van was now heading straight toward a brick building that looked like the same one I had been held in. But then, knowing there was no way I was going to survive that, I did the only thing I could think to do. So, I grabbed the wheel, turning it far too quickly and making the van tip onto two wheels before flipping over. I had no option but to let go of the wheel and felt my whole body free falling for a split second, before pain erupted as I was slammed into the side window. I then ended up flipped upside down until the whole thing stilled enough for me to ask myself what just happened.

One side of my face felt wet, and when I moved, pain radiated from my temple. I moved my limbs one by one, thankful nothing was broken but just tender. Although this wasn't the end of my problems as the windscreen was shot at before someone was kicking it in, making glass burst around me.

"AHHH!" I screamed before one of Gomez's men was reaching inside and dragging me out by my ankle, making me realize that I had hurt myself more than I'd thought. My ankle hurt enough to tell me it was likely a sprain, something that was confirmed when I was forced to my feet and had to put weight on it.

"Fuck!" I hissed, before trying to pull out of the grip one of them had on my arm, using it to drag me along.

"I will put a bullet in your head, bitch. I get paid no matter what, but Gomez wanted you alive so I would go with that option if I were you!" the big man said, gripping me painfully. He had a thick moustache, a square head and a buzz cut that screamed military. He was also the one the others were following, which probably meant that he was the one in charge of this new team of men. Men that would soon find out they were suicidal to even consider taking on this job.

But until such time came that they could realize the colossal fuck up they were making, I let them lead me back into the building I recognized from the van. We were at the warehouse the furthest away from where Ward and the others were still fighting, making me wonder if this was where the girls were being held? We were entering it at a different side to where I had come out of, so I was trying to map it out in my mind. Something that was difficult as a lot of the buildings all looked the same and the place was so big, it was hard to keep track.

"When will the chopper get here?" one of the other men asked, and I swear that all the guys wearing black were starting to merge into one! But there was one major difference between the bad guys and who I was considering the murderous good...

Size.

Each of Hel's men were tall and buff, looking like they lived in a gym and worked out twenty-four seven. Especially Hel, but then he was clearly the one in charge. Speaking of which, I was really hoping that rescue number two was in the making as the word chopper didn't exactly mean good things.

"Gomez is waiting to be picked up first, over on the West side, so we need to get to the roof," soldier boy in charge informed the others as we made our way through a pair of roller doors, that first had been opened with the use of bolt cutters. Then, with a team of eight all surrounding me, I was led further inside while two others closed the doors, locking them shut.

I didn't recognize the place but seeing as we were now inside what looked like a loading bay, then it wasn't surprising. Besides, one warehouse just looked like the next, so what did I know? Crates were stacked around us with some pallets wrapped up in plastic sheeting that were full of God knows what. A few empty broken pallets remained propped up against the wall, which was the extent of what this large open space held.

"Wait, what the fuck was that?!" one of the men said when he heard a noise behind us, making them all turn their guns back to the roller doors we'd just entered through. The two closest started to walk back to regroup, no doubt feeling they had strength in numbers. That's when the banging started, and the metal caved inwards, as if it had been hit with a fist-sized wrecking ball.

"Look alive, men, we have another asshole to deal with," the one in charge said before tossing me behind them, making me go stumbling into the side of one of the crates. But despite this, I was frozen by the sight of the doors being hammered against, and the sound grew louder and louder. I slowly shifted my feet, ignoring the pain in my ankle so I could try and find myself some protection against whatever was coming next, until suddenly a Demonic fist emerged, making me scream.

The doors were then pealed back, like creating a doorway in metal was as easy as cutting foil. After this new doorway was big enough, in walked a man who changed with every step he made into something beyond terrifying. That was when I realized that the barest glimpse I had witnessed before was nothing compared to this!

He was a monster!

Crimson red mottled skin was bursting with jagged horns like carved rock, outlining his body as they travelled like a spine up his arms, shoulders and neck. His veins seemed to rise to the surface, pumping liquid fire, the demonic glow pulsating just beneath the hard skin. His eyes were completely black, like staring into two onyx stones that lacked all emotion. Blood branched out around his eyes and the edges of his Demonic face, like a snake's forked tongue, lashing out at his own skin.

The rest of his huge body was made of sections of glowing armor plating, and horns surrounded by rough hard skin, making it hard to know where the warrior ended and where the Demon began.

I sucked back a gasp, finding myself soon pressed against a wall with my palms flat against the cool brick. The pain in my ankle was throbbing but I was determined to stay on my feet, despite being terrified. Because I didn't know this man, *this Demon.* Making me truly realize now my biggest mistake…

I didn't know enough about Ward's world.

I had also forgotten to tell Ward about what Gomez had said about there being two people who wanted to pay for me. Was this the other guy? What if he was and he was here now to take me by force, seizing his opportunity, getting me for free while everyone else was busy fighting each other?

But then, what could such a beast want with me?

I didn't get a chance to consider this for long as the second the Demon walked fully inside, he spoke.

"I hope you fuckers are harder to kill this time, *I hate it when my prey is eager to die."* He said this last part in a Demonic growl, and I shivered. The feeling of dread soon turned into screaming when all Hell broke loose and guns were fired as one in his direction. At this I couldn't help it, I dropped to the floor and covered my head with my hands, hoping this could save me from the onslaught of ricocheting bullets. But then one guy was suddenly thrown and hit the wall next to me, making me scream. It also forced me to stop cowering as I was forced to look to see the slaughter for myself. Because that was exactly what it was.

A massacre.

His Demonic body moved so quickly, it was like watching the whole room after it had been recorded and someone had hit the fast forward button, doing so while the rest of the world was left trying to play catch up. He was lashing out with his deadly claws, making blood spray up from a mercenary's chest cavity, having cut through whatever armor he may have worn. Because there was no such thing as protection against this beast.

I watched as one man unleashed bullet after bullet from his automatic weapon, screaming in rage as he did. As for the Demon, he seemed to bring forth a Hellish chest plate, that was swirls of interlocking red rock, and looked as if it had been carved by the Devil himself.

It was also one that had put up an impenetrable barrier between himself and the raining assault of bullets. This meant that he was free to continue to walk toward the mercenary, at the same time the guy walked backward, still firing his weapon. Doing so, despite it having zero effect on him. Because there was one problem with this for the guy with the gun, he would soon run out of bullets, which is precisely what he did. Which meant that when it finished, the Demon simply grinned and said,

"My turn." Then he grabbed the long weapon, and literally snapped it in half before using both pieces to impale the guy to the wall he had backed up into. I hissed before trying to keep down the urge to vomit as blood oozed out of him. Then, while leaving this victim to die, he turned side on at just the right time. This was so he could catch the next one by the neck, as he

had been running at him with a knife raised high. He lifted the guy three feet into the air before twisting his wrist and snapping his neck like it had been made from a brittle twig.

But then, while he had been doing this, another guy had crept up out of nowhere and was about to fire at point blank range at his head. Seeing this and I don't know why, but something in me just snapped. As if this Demon suddenly meant something on a deeper level. So I acted before I could give it an ounce of thought, suddenly screaming so loud, it was with every fiber of my being! Yet this time, I also knew the root of it wasn't fear.

It was anger.

It was also so powerful that it made the man drop his gun and instantly try to cover his ears, that I briefly noticed were bleeding. Then he dropped to the floor after his eyes had rolled back up into his head as if I had just…

Killed him.

I gasped in shock, looking first to the dead guy and then to the Demon who was now staring at me. I started to back away, knowing there was a door around here, doing so in case he was going be angry. However, he cocked his head to the side and muttered,

"So, I am worthy." I frowned at this, not understanding why he said it or what he even meant by it. The only thing I could deduce, was that my scream hadn't affected him as it had done to the dead merc on the ground, making me wonder if he thought it should have.

I didn't get much time to figure this out as I was still terrified. I turned quickly the moment I felt the wall run out, meaning I had finally found the doorway. However, the second I turned, I was faced with a gun being pointed at my head, as Mr. square jaw who had dragged me in here was back. He must have made a run for it to try and find back up when the massacre started. Now clearly, he had decided to take a different approach. As he must have had figured out his only way of escape was to use me as a hostage. I knew this the second he grabbed me to him, spun me around to face the Demon and promptly put...

His gun to my head.

CHAPTER 13

EXPLOSIVE TIMES

"No! Get off me!" I shouted as soon as I was grabbed and spun around. He had a handgun to the side of my head, making his intentions clear.

"Shut the fuck up!" he snapped, digging the end of the barrel into my temple. The Demon, who still held the dead man dangling in his grasp, narrowed his deadly gaze dangerously. Then he simply tossed his kill to the side as if he was a piece of dirty laundry before he began to stalk closer. I could feel the gun shaking against the side of my temple and I wasn't surprised in the slightest, as the Demon was fucking terrifying! Hell, I think I was close to hearing this guy's damn heartbeat as it was clear he was petrified and in truth, he wasn't the only one.

"Don't come any closer or I will shoot this bitch!" the man shouted, making the Demon take pause. Then, with a slight narrowing of his eyes, this time centered on his gun, he asked,

"With what?"

Even I frowned at the question, not understanding it. As for the soldier, he shifted the weapon enough that I was free to turn my head, and his look of confusion was soon mirroring my own. Because we both watched as the gun started to evaporate into millions of tiny pieces, almost like metal sand that was caught up in the wind. At this, the man panicked and grabbed me by throat, squeezing it until I couldn't breathe.

"I don't need a gun to kill this bitch, now back the fuck off!" I started to panic, reaching up now, trying desperately to get his fingers off me. As for the Demon, he simply homed in on his hand around my neck and shrugged his shoulders.

"Just as I don't need my hands to break yours," he replied calmly, just as the man started screaming in agony at the same time that I felt the pressure being released from my neck. I nearly fell forward but caught myself at the last second, turning to find the man backing away, clutching his clearly broken fingers to his chest. I felt sick when I saw the way they were all bent back toward the top of his palm. It was as if they had been broken in so many different places, it was nothing more than a mangled mess of broken bones held inside his flesh.

I quickly got out of the way, limping to find a place I could hide, and when I saw some crates stacked in the corner, I slipped behind them and tried to make myself as small as possible. I didn't know what the guy wanted with me or if he was indeed one of the good guys. No, the only thing I knew for sure was that I had just witnessed him take out all these guys in no more than two minutes.

Something he had seemed to enjoy immensely.

He had played with his prey. I knew that the second he made that gun disappear, knowing he could have done that from the start. But he hadn't, meaning he had made a game of killing. He hadn't wanted to make it too easy.

I held my hands over my ears to try and drown out the screaming of the man who now sounded as though he was having his insides torn out while he was being made to watch. I wondered then if he had saved this bloodier death until I couldn't watch? If so, I at least had that to be thankful for before I was to be his next victim. Although, this seemed unlikely, which was why I tried to fight my fearful mind with facts. Because why go to all the trouble of killing the men that had me, if he had only wanted to add me to his death count?

Unless he enjoyed the chase.

No, Edie, get a grip, the Demon beast man is trying to save your life, not eat you! At this thought, I heard chuckling, making me suddenly realize that he most likely could hear my thoughts like the rest of Ward's pals could. Great, way to piss off the big man, seriously, why don't I just think of pulling a big steak from my non-existent purse and throwing it at him…? Oh my God, there I go again! Why couldn't I just stop? Christmas… think of Christmas, not that I have any plans, being kind of homeless and all… no, stop, lalalala… jingle bells, jungle bells…

"As amusing as your mind is, I must put a stop to it now and insist you come with me," his deep voice said, making me shiver as the authority of it blanketed me with dominance. Like my submissive nature was begging me to do as he asked as his command wrapped itself around me. But then I jumped the second the crate was moved, revealing my crummy hiding space.

"I will not hurt you, little Siren." He gentled his voice, making me look up and quickly realize he was the large man from when Ward had first emerged with me in his arms. I hadn't recognized him in his Demon form because Ward had protected me from watching what happened with his wings.

"It's you!" I exclaimed somewhat stupidly, making him grin and I had to say… wow. It was one that totally transformed his face from badass to ruggedly handsome in a heartbeat. In fact, he looked like some modern-day Viking warrior that had just stepped off a boat. However, I wasn't so quick to let go of the petrifying side of him I had seen, so couldn't help but flinch when he took a step toward me.

Jesus, but what was it with these guys, did they model for supernatural calendars each year? At this he burst out laughing and I covered my mouth with my hand as if I had spoken aloud, when it was my mind that was the problem.

"I confess, it has been a while since I stepped off a boat," he said with a wink, and I think it was done as a way to help me relax around him.

"I am a friend of Ward's... my name is Wrath," he told me, making me frown a little.

"Wrath?" I questioned on a gulp, thinking it wasn't exactly the friendliest name I had ever heard. But then again, just looking at the guy and well, I couldn't imagine him with a name like Jim or Bert. But then his lips quirked, fighting another grin as it was clear I was basically shouting out these thoughts in his mind.

"Kaiden Wrath, my friends call me Kai if that helps ease your fears," he said, holding out his hand for me to take.

"Well, it isn't Jim but it's better than Mr. Angry," I replied, putting my hand in his and feeling tiny when I did. Again, he burst out laughing, a booming sound that echoed in the large open space. Then he helped me to my feet, and he told me,

"You are a delight, and I can see why my friend is so intent on burning this place to the ground in your honor."

"Erm... thanks, *I think,*" I muttered, making him chuckle. Then I heard screaming and this time, it wasn't from one of Wrath's victims.

It was a girl's scream.

"Oh God! Come on, we have to save them!" I shouted, now trying to limp toward the only door that must have led into the rooms at the back of the warehouse. I didn't get far before a meaty hand stopped me.

"What girls?"

"Gomez had girls held prisoner and we have to save them before..." I didn't even want to finish that sentence. Wrath narrowed his eyes a second before he held a finger to his ear and started issuing orders in the hidden ear piece there.

"Hel, tell Ward I've got his girl, she is safe, but I need a team here for extraction, multiple female hostages. One minute," he said before cutting the communication.

"Hel, he was fighting with the others," I commented, remembering the name.

"He's my brother... now do you think you can show me where these girls are?" I nodded, after showing a moment of surprise at hearing the two were related... they looked nothing alike.

"Two rules, stay close to me and do as I say... yes?" he told me and I gave him a salute for some unknown reason, but my nervousness was making me act irrational.

"Cute... now let's go," he commented, making me blush as he took my hand and started to lead me through the door.

"You're limping. I don't scent blood but tell me now if you are injured?" he said, stopping me.

"I must have just sprained my ankle but it's nothing I can't deal with."

"Then I will carry you," he said, taking a step toward me as if he was about to take me in his arms.

"No, no, it's fine... I promise I am fine to walk, besides, I have a feeling they will need you more," I told him after taking a step back, making him frown down at me. He looked torn in his decision before he nodded once.

"Alright, but if it gets too painful then you must tell me."

"Deal," I agreed, making him smirk. We continued walking but when someone appeared behind us, I was shifted and before this new enemy could even get a shot off, Wrath reached up and drew a long black spike from under his skin. It was one that had already started protruding up through his flesh, making it easy for him to grip on to. He yanked it out and threw it like a throwing knife, hitting the man in the chest and knocking him clean off his feet.

"Holy shit!" I couldn't help but shout. It was as cool as it was shocking. As for Wrath, he simply held out his hand and the horn shot to his hand before he stabbed it back inside his body without even a flinch. This whole thing happened in no more than three seconds flat, and I was left looking up at him with my mouth agape. Then he tapped me under the chin with a little chuckle.

"That was… erm… impressive," I stuttered, making him wink down at me. Then he took my hand in his again and started pulling me along with him as we made our way through the labyrinth of rooms and hallways.

"I hear them!" I shouted, and just before I could take off running, I was stopped with a stern order.

"Stay here." Then he stepped around the next corner to go and investigate. This was when I heard footsteps. I turned around quickly and when I saw more soldiers coming at us, I ran for Wrath, bumping into his back.

"I hope you've got a lot more horns, Spikey. I think you're going to need them." At this he grinned down at me.

"Spikey?" he questioned, making me shrug before commenting,

"If the shoes fits… holy mother of God, just how big are your feet!?" I asked, blurting it out and making him boom with laughter again, telling me with a knowing grin,

"There is no mother of a God to thank, of that you can be certain." Then he tucked me close behind him before rounding the corner back the way we came, to face whatever the next threat was.

"I don't know which to address first, the reason you're showing the poor girl your feet or why she has nicknamed you Spikey," Hel commented when coming into view and pulling the tactical helmet from his head, making me sigh in relief at the sight of the cavalry. He led a group of five men, meaning we were now eight in total, making the hallway look cramped.

"You are simply sour because where I am concerned, size is all relative, *little brother,*" Wrath said, making his point and slapping Hel on the back, and I giggled at the jest.

"What've we got, Kai?" Hel asked getting back to business.

"I can detect at least seven heartbeats and the scent of the women held in the cells ahead. But the rest of the building has been cleared. Where is Ward?" he asked, making me step up to Hel and grab his arm, asking,

"Is he alright?!"

"It takes a lot more to kill that hard bastard," he commented, making me frown up at him.

"Helmer." Wrath said his brother's name as a kind of warning, but also letting me know now why his name was Hel.

"I apologize, little one. Your Enforcer is fine and currently hunting Gomez after catching sight of him trying to make a run for it." I released a breath and told them both,

"He's got a chopper coming, I overheard the men talking about it. The plan was to get me to the roof after Gomez was picked up." It was in that moment that something could be heard above, and all the men looked up.

"Sounds like it's here," Hel commented.

"We will have to leave that in Ward's hands. Our priority now is to get the girls out of here," Wrath said in a stern tone.

"Agreed," Hel said, directing his men down there. I took a step to follow but was promptly held back by Wrath.

"Please let me go with them, those girls have been through Hell by the hands of men... they will all be terrified," I told him, making him look first to the way his men had come and then back to my pleading eyes. I knew he was trying to weigh up his options but then something in my eyes must have been enough to sway him as he nodded.

He walked close to me as we made our way to the cells he had obviously seen and when I heard the screams of terror, I ran, slipping loose from his relaxed grip easily.

"Siren!" Wrath shouted, obviously not knowing me by anything else, but it didn't matter, I just wanted to help save them as I myself had been saved. But then this was where things got bad, as I could see the very last cell at the end of the hallway I remembered being walked down. The difference however, was when the door was opened by one of Wrath's men, the whole room blew up as if it had been rigged to do so. The door flew into a block wall opposite with the force of the explosion, knocking the man back before he was able to use his own abilities at being able to control the blaze.

"NO!" I screamed in horror, thinking of the poor soul that had been held in there. Then I was picked up from behind and turned, as if to protect me as one of his men contained the flames in an invisible ball of energy. The sounds of his men barking orders were barely heard over the girls' screams, their frightened cries now near deafening. But one sound that started to drown it all out was that of the helicopter.

A helicopter that seemed to be getting closer overhead... too close in fact.

Wrath looked up and then a second later roared,

"GET DOWN!"

And then everything around us...

Exploded.

CHAPTER 14
WHEN DEATH KNOCKS
WARD

"*Come back to me, Ward...*"

Eden's words played over and over in my mind, even as I fought the next wave of mercenaries that had been sent to attack us. It made me wonder, just how many of these guys did Gomez hope to lose in this fight, just so it was a smaller bill to pay?

Well, he was soon to pay with his life, for there was no way I was letting that fucker leave here alive! But my first priority was to get Eden out of here. I ordered Deke to take care of it, giving them the all clear to do that by taking out the group trying to get shots at the van. I had taken to the sky and directed my Darkness toward the ground so that when I landed it shot out around me, forcing those with guns to fly backward.

But they weren't the only dead underlings to deal with, as the next wave came shooting from around the corner, making me throw up my wings to protect my vessel as I didn't have time to fucking heal it right away. Then I felt for every heartbeat in that area, and taking the time needed to concentrate my Darkness, I lashed out all at once. My power entered into

103

their bodies and crushed their hearts with each arm of death my vengeance produced.

It was a difficult move but an effective one, as I knew that by the time I moved my wings back, the eight men would be lying dead on the floor, all falling as one the moment my Darkness released them. But unfortunately, this wasn't the only thing I saw when I pulled back my wings. First there was Deke, who had been caught trying to protect the van from snipers as it drove away.

Had one of Hel's men got behind the wheel at his orders? I had to be sure, as the van was already heading toward the gates. But then the second it started to swerve toward one of the warehouses, I sucked back a startled breath and reached out my mind to discover who was driving.

"NO!" I roared in fury before stretching my wings and flying down, fully intent on getting her.

I should have just flown her right out of here myself and left my vengeance for another day! Fuck! But I should have put her first and ignored my nature's need for revenge. *I should have done more!*

I should have... Boom! A fucking rocket launcher just targeted me without me knowing it, as my head was far from fucking clear trying to get to her. I was hit and my body went spiraling out of control, twisting up in my wings as I landed into the side of a building with a jarring impact. I must have blacked out for a few seconds, as the popping of my bones making their way back into place after they had pierced through my flesh, woke me with a start.

"Seriously, just how many times do I have to drag your ass out from underneath a fucking building?" Deke's voice brought me back the rest of the way, as he was indeed dragging me from the rubble my impact had caused.

"Eden!" I shouted when the reasons for my flight hit me.

"Wrath is there, he will save her." I snarled at this, as there was only one man who should be saving her and that was fucking me! Which was why I cracked my dislocated shoulder back into place and called forth my wings again, fully intent on getting to her myself when Deke stopped me.

"Gomez, Ward, you need to cut the head off the snake to fully end this!"

"No, what I need is my girl!" I barked back before shrugging off his hold.

"Then she will never be safe until you do, and what will happen next time, because it won't be money he asks for... it will be redemption." This made me take pause. My head snapped back to his and he dragged a hand over his head, telling me what I needed to hear to end this.

"Gomez might not be in the wind for long before we find him, but what if it's long enough to try this again. What if the next fucking rocket doesn't hit you but is aimed at...?"

"Don't fucking say it!" I snarled, fucking hating that he was right! This might be my one opportunity to get this fucker once and for all. Because I couldn't chance this happening again. I couldn't chance something worse. I couldn't chance her life. I looked toward the warehouse, seeing the van now on its roof, knowing something had happened. I took a step forward as if by instinct, but I allowed my friend's words to stop me again.

"I saw her from a distance, they got her out and took her inside. Wrath followed seconds later. Trust me on this, Ward, he will save her." I released a sigh, knowing he was right. Wrath would kill every last fucker before they even had chance to lay a finger on her to cause harm. But as for me, I couldn't waste this opportunity to end this once and for all.

"Fuck!" I hissed, balling my fists before turning back to my friend.

"Fine... Let's go get this fucker!" I growled, cracking the

last of my broken knuckles back into place, looking toward the only building left and seeing now the helicopter far in the distance that was his obvious escape plan.

"Ward!" Hel approached, looking bloody, unsurprisingly, none of which was his own. But it looked as if his men were fanning out to dispatch the running cowards.

"Your brother, he was…"

"She is safe, Kai just told me he has her. We are making our way there now." The second I heard this my hand shot to Deke's shoulder as the emotion near brought me to my knees.

"Thank the Gods!" I muttered after feeling as if my heart would beat its way out my fucking chest!

"Eden mentioned something about girls," I told him, making him nod.

"Kai is looking for them now with your girl. We are going to help get them out. I take it you will be hunting?" Hel added this last part nodding toward the tallest building, and the one soldier boy had died pointing to.

"Vengeance will be mine," I growled.

"Then let me give you a crumb to follow. He and a few of his men were seen running into the building on the west side. It looks as if it's been under construction." I nodded my thanks, making him respond,

"Happy hunting, my friend, and don't worry about your girl, we will keep her safe. Let's go, gentlemen!" he said, ending this by ordering his team into the vehicles they had arrived in, minus one after it had been shot to shit and now lay tipped up on its roof.

As for Deke and I, we both released our wings and were landing in front of the building Hel had mentioned within seconds.

"So, we got a plan here?" Deke asked after landing next to me just as his wings had started to disappear. I narrowed my gaze on the building, concentrating on the heartbeats inside. Then, when I found the biggest group, with one beating erratically in the center of them all, I knew I had got him.

"Found you, fucker!" I snarled before telling Deke, "Enter through the floor below and draw their fire, I will enter above and cut them off, picking off the few he will keep with him to get him to the roof. We have two minutes before that bird lands... go!" He nodded with a grin, calling back his wings once more and making his entrance as loud as possible, letting them know he was coming. He did this by flying up to the floor I instructed he enter at and after first curling his wings around him, he catapulted himself through the glass. The window burst around him as his body disappeared, making as much noise as he could.

As for myself, I took a far stealthier approach, using my Darkness to attach onto the window and pull it toward me. This was so the glass would only break when it hit the ground. A sound that wouldn't have been heard from inside. Not when it would still be drowned out by what little were left of Gomez's army. The ones still left fighting the half of Hel's men he had left to clean up the scraps.

So knowing this, I simply stepped inside, allowing my wings to disappear the moment my foot was on the ledge and my hand was on the window frame. I folded my large frame inside and quickly scanned the area, taking in the sound of gunfire below as Deke was obviously doing his job. And from the sound of the screams, I would say he was doing it well.

Just like I knew he would.

I closed my eyes for a second, trying to pinpoint what I now recognized as Gomez's dark heart, feeling it coming closer. This floor, like the rest of the building, was in the process of being renovated, I could smell the fresh paint and drywall dust on the floor. Plastic sheeting had been used to prevent this from getting into completed offices, making me wonder just what Gomez was intending to use this building for? Another front for his drug running perhaps.

But then my Siren's face entered my mind, and with every fiber of my being did I want to fly straight out of this window and find her. To ensure she was in fact safe, and make sure what Hel told me was true. That Wrath had got to her in time.

I snarled silently, curling my lip and letting my fangs grow, frustrated that it couldn't yet be a roar of fury. No, I didn't want that fucker knowing I was here waiting for him, ready to strike when he least expected it. So, I let my Darkness seep in around me, hiding me in the shadows of my vengeance as I allowed a sheet of plastic to fall in place. From the other side, I knew it would have looked like a window into Hell with the Reaper there to welcome him.

In no time at all, as expected, the panicked sounds of Gomez and his few remaining foot soldiers burst through onto this floor as the staircase to the roof was found on this level. I had purposely positioned myself so they would have to walk by me and the second they did, I would start picking them off one by one.

I looked up as the last man passed me, deciding this would be the first of my victims and exactly how he would go. Then I let my Darkness rise above me into the false ceiling so it could take the merc from above. It snatched him from the floor in less time than it took him to scream and held him suspended there.

"What the fuck?!" one said, catching the movement and before questioning anything, the fools all started shooting up at the ceiling just like I knew they would. This therefore meant that they ended up doing the killing for me, as they shot their own man. I grinned to myself as I released my hold on him, so they could see for themselves what they'd done.

He landed, causing a cloud of dust to rise around him, and I got a sick satisfaction seeing the way the newly laid floor was now stained crimson.

"Fuck! What the fuck was that!?" Gomez yelled, only making my grin grow. Because I could tell him exactly what it was...

It was the sound of death coming for him.

CHAPTER 15
CONSUMED

"How the fuck did he get picked up like that?!" One of the mercs asked, now pointing his weapon erratically at too many points in the room as if looking for a ghost. Well, he was about to find more than a fucking ghost!

"I told you, these fuckers aren't human!" another said, and a second man added,

"I saw that one guy jump his way up a fucking building, practically took out the other team!" The last man who stood in front of Gomez, who was leading point on this extraction, sliced his arm down in the air and hissed,

"Shut the fuck up, all of you! Now fan out, I want..."

"Fuck that! You're paid to protect me!" Gomez argued after grabbing the asshole, who I gathered was in charge of yet another unit of mercenaries he had paid to die. He yanked himself free of Gomez's near-death grip and snapped,

"Fine, tight formation, stay close and grow eyes out your fucking assholes!"

Little good it would do them, I thought with a dark grin. I then held out my hands to the floor, commanding my essence to escape from under my skin until it was a thick fog rolling around their feet like a silent wave. And they didn't even notice, too busy looking to where they expected to find me.

I let the fog rise until it was just about to reach their knees then suddenly, I let it take hold of two of them, yanking them from standing and dragging them into the mist screaming. The remaining two started shooting pointlessly again into my Darkness, making me laugh. A sadistic sound that echoed throughout the open space, making the newly installed glass in the windows rattle before cracking.

"Fuck this, Sarge! I am not dying for this fucker!" one of the last remining men said, before trying to hurry for the exit. But if he thought I was letting one of my victims go so easily, then he was delusional. Which was why I grabbed him out of sight, plucking him off the floor and holding him by the throat. However, when I looked into his heart, it wasn't as black as all the rest.

No, what I was seeing now was nothing more than a traumatized mind, scarred through shitty circumstances. He had been affected by war but discharged for denying a direct order to kill someone he didn't think should be killed. Someone who got punished despite this heroic attempt at saving a life instead of taking it. He got kicked out of the army. Dishonorable discharge, which was a term used and was anything but, in my eyes, as he had been right, the girl had been innocently looking for refuge. However, only one had wanted to take that chance on her, despite the bomb someone had strapped to her chest. Tears pleading for someone to help her. Offering up the detonator, begging for a way out of her life.

He had wanted that for her.

He dreamt of her every night.

Bitterness had taken hold but that was about it. He came home after losing everything only to find himself losing even more. Disgraced by his own family, he joined this band of rejects and hoped to make a difference. But then his Sarge had got greedy, taking jobs for shitheads like Gomez. People this Mark didn't believe were good enough to protect. It was why Mark had aimed all his shots not to kill but to wound.

It was also why Mark would be the only survivor this day.

I placed my hand over his temple and let the visions of how he could choose flow through. To either die by my hands this very day or show him his first glimpse of the life he could still have, should he want to survive.

"The girl is in a better place, so let her go and live your own life, for you are walking along someone else's path of destruction and not journeying to the salvation you deserve to reach," I whispered in his head, before leaving my mark of protection upon him, one he would always feel but never see. Then I let him go and told him,

"Your friends will not be so lucky, so I suggest... *you start running."* Something he wisely did after first making the sign of Christ, making me chuckle to myself.

"Good boy, Mark." I uttered darkly as I drew my Darkness back to my being, seeing as there was only two left protecting Gomez. Two dark souls left to collect, and then Gomez was mine. I took control of the mind of Sarge, who turned his gun on his own soldier, and in a voice that was not his own, told him,

"Are you afraid of dying?"

"Sarge?" he replied in an unsure tone, looking at the gun pointing his way, making Gomez snap,

"Oh, fuck this shit!" Then the fat little shit ran for the door that would lead him up to the roof, and I listened out to hear the chopper getting closer, knowing now I didn't have long. I walked out of the shadows and just as the soldier raised his gun to take me out, I made a fist with my hand, making the his gun fold in around his hand, crushing it in a mangle of metal and bone.

He started screaming and I clicked my fingers, making the one I had under my control shoot him in the head. Then, to my minion, I nodded to the door and told him to precede me.

"After you." He walked up first, and I saw Gomez there waving his arms like the chubby fucker was trying to fly. I purposely walked directly behind him so Gomez wouldn't see me at first, seeing that this guy was at the very least my height.

"Tell me you finally found the asshole!" Gomez snapped, waving the chopper over now. But when the guy didn't answer, Gomez finally took a closer look and I kicked in the sergeant's legs, so he landed on his knees. Then I released my hold over his mind so he could feel the terror of what was about to happen. Which meant that now he was at the right height, I took his head in a hold and told Gomez,

"No, but the asshole very much found you!" Then I snapped his neck, and kept my muscles working enough to rip his head from his body, so I could throw it at my enemy's feet, doing so with a long streak of blood lining the floor. Gomez's stunned eyes looked down at the proof I was not a man to be fucked with.

In fact, I was not a man at all.

I was a Reaper of the Gods.

"Wh-what... the fu-fu-fuck... are y-you?" he stammered, walking backward and to give him his due, he didn't vomit or empty his bowels like I thought he would. I started walking forward and within a blink of his eyes, I was there right in front of him by the time he opened them again.

"AHH!" he hollered in fright, as I grabbed him by the throat and raised him up.

"I'm your executioner!" But then, just before I could start ripping him apart, one small piece at a time, he fumbled for his

pocket before finding something he thought could be used against me. I knew this when I felt something cold slap against my face and before I could laugh at the absurdity of it all, its power suddenly hit me, making my Darkness grimace.

I ended up throwing him across the rooftop and not because I wanted to make his terror of me last. But the attempt at hurting me had actually... *worked.*

However, I knew from the look of shock on his face just before I tossed him backward, that he had been led to believe it would do a lot more. Maybe it would have had he held it to my skin for longer. But as it was, it fell to the ground.

As for Gomez, he went skidding across the tiles, made slippery from all the blood that poured out of the dead Sargent's body, landing next to it. I calmly bent down, seeing now that it was some kind of ancient amulet that he had kept wrapped up in a piece of red velvet cloth. I wrapped it back up, and picked it up, feeling the weight of its power in my hand but knowing that unless it touched my bare skin, I was unaffected. I pocketed the item before walking back toward Gomez. I then kicked the head aside before stalking my victim once more, when he suddenly grabbed the man's automatic weapon.

I started laughing when he struggled to his feet and took aim. I then opened my arms and released my wings, letting him see as I allowed my Darkness to possess my body, changing me back into my true nature.

"You really think you can kill me! I warned you not to fuck with me. Now it's time to pay the price, Felix Gomez... *Now it's time to face your sins!*" I said, letting my Darkness speak this last part and with shaky hands, he lifted the weapon as he had no choice for anything else at this point. He started firing and I raised my wings to deflect them, just as I felt the helicopter flying in overhead.

But this was where I fucked up.

As his bullets may not have been able to harm me, but that's not to say they didn't do damage. The spray of projectiles hit the engine, causing the helicopter to start flying out of control, making it veer to one side and head straight for the only fucking place I didn't want it to go!

I quickly cast my hands out to it, and with as much strength as I had, I held it suspended, feeling my powers slipping thanks to the relic that had the power to absorb them, taking them from me. I felt the strain of keeping it steady but just before I could start bringing it down, I felt a slight motion in my pocket and then suddenly, that same pain against the back of my neck. It instantly rendered me powerless for a split second, but that was all it took!

"NO!" I roared as I was forced to watch as the helicopter flew from my grasp and crashed sideways into the building I knew Eden was in. Rage exploded inside me as I spun and grabbed Gomez, ripping the amulet out of his hand, wrapping it around my fist. Then, without thought of pain or suffering or my dark job to serve the Gods, without even vengeance,

I punched my hand into his torso and grabbed hold of his intestines. Then I took a step back and as he looked down at his own death, shocked to see it spilling out of him, I said,

"For Eden!" Then I kicked him off the roof, holding on to his intestines so that they unraveled out of him until he reached the end and hit the ground. Then I let go and released my wings so I could fly over to the building.

One that was now…

Consumed by flames.

CHAPTER 16

CONTROLLING FIRE
EDEN

Fire.

Fire and screaming.

That's what I remember as the helicopter tore its way through the building. But that wasn't all I remembered, as I was tossed out of the way. This, I was to discover later, was as half the warehouse I had first been dragged into started to collapse in on itself. But it didn't stop there, as I could still remember the smell of the fuel before I even had chance to open my eyes to take in the damage.

But this replay of events now felt more like a dream, making me wonder if I had died.

No, I couldn't have, as I remembered more after this.

I opened my eyes and after watching Wrath pulling himself from part of the damaged wall, his eyes quickly found mine. But then as he started to make his way to me, he sniffed the air, before his wide eyes told me he knew what was coming. Hence why he ordered,

"The place is going to blow! Teko, short the bombs and get the girls out, THEN MOVE!" Then he roared this last part of his order before picking me up off the floor. He followed his men who were now, like Wrath, soon carrying unconscious women in their arms. This was while I noticed one man who looked to be casting some kind of spell on the doors. I recognized him as being the same man who had thrown up a shield outside and had saved us from being hit by the second attack. Well, it looked as if he was back at it, as he was obviously stopping the doors from blowing like the first had, making his way along before one of the men stepped inside and saved another girl.

"The plans showed there is another loading bay on the other side!" one of his men at the front said, making Wrath nod for him to lead the way. But seeing as we were at the back, we were the ones affected the most when the helicopter finally exploded after some spark must have found its way to the fuel spewing out of it. Wrath, thinking fast, threw me into one of the cells and slammed the door, trying to save me as the explosion caused fire to travel through the hallway.

I screamed, covering my head as I could see flames just outside the door, cutting off my escape. I couldn't help but hope they had managed to get the girls to safety but also, that Wrath too had been uninjured in the blast. Because if he had been, then he had sacrificed his own life to save mine! And from the looks of the flames outside my door, it looked to be in vain if that was the case.

Because I was now trapped.

I could see the smoke coming in from under the door, which soon had me coughing, and I tried to cover my mouth with my hand as I looked around for something more. I grabbed a pillowcase, knowing it was impractical to use the sheets as they would be too big to carry around with me. That was, if I ever had a chance at getting out of here!

I started coughing harder now, as the room was filling with more smoke. I ran to the bathroom and doused the material in water, knowing this would help when covering my mouth. But by the time this was done, I knew it had been pointless as more of the room was covered in smoke. I wouldn't last long.

But then, just before I could give up hope as I was far too close to passing out, the door suddenly opened and a Demonic figure appeared through the flames.

"Wrath!" I tried to shout his name, reaching a hand out to him, now knowing that seeing him in his other form didn't scare me anymore. I watched wide-eyed as he started to draw in the blazing fire behind him, as if he was the very source of it all! He was commanding it, pulling it closer until flames licked at his body before being absorbed inside him.

It wasn't like watching a candle dying down slowly until it was gone. It was more like watching the larges flames sink into his flesh and simply disappear. He continued to do this until the very last of the fire behind him was gone, before he raised up a hand and concentrated on the smoke in the room. He drew it in, absorbing it, making me cough out as I tried to drag clean air back into my lungs, making them burn from the effort.

This was when he stepped inside and picked me up, now cradling my body to his massive chest, making me feel small and weak. Something I had to admit in that moment, I was.

"Your Enforcer will heal you soon, just keep breathing for me and live or Ward will kill me if I deliver you dead," he said, and his tone suggested he was teasing. I laughed in return but started coughing, making him frown at me.

"Don't... make... me laugh!" I wheezed out, making him grin.

"I will try my best, Eden." He surprised me by knowing my name, which was when I told him,

"Call... me... Edie." He winked at me, but this was the last thing I remember saying to him as I closed my eyes and felt my world fade from flames...

To black.

ⴲ

"Eden... come back to me, my Siren." The moment I heard his voice, it was like a beacon guiding me home. As if my subconscious mind was chasing for it and suddenly, there I was, running along a beach. He had something in his hand right in front of me, teasing me with it...

A gift.

I was laughing and so was he.

We were, *finally, happy together.*

Which was when he let me have it, making me reach out at the same time he wrapped an arm around me and pulled me close. Then just was as I was about to open the gift, he whispered in my ear what it truly held inside...

His heart.

I woke with a start and right into Ward's arms, as he pulled me close.

"Ward, you're okay... you're okay," I said on a thankful sigh, totally relieved to be in his arms again. He held me close, cradling my head to his neck, and I wondered why I could taste blood.

"She's asking me if I am okay... Gods, girl, but you and your sweetness could bring me to my knees," he told me, after saying this first part to himself and making me grin against his neck. But then, while I tried to pull back, I noticed the blood left on his neck. I reached up to my lips and gave him wide, questioning eyes.

"I needed to heal you as you were struggling to breathe with all the smoke." I frowned as I searched for the memories, and that's when it hit me... I had been in the cell about to die.

Wrath had saved me.

"Wrath! Is he alright?" I asked, making Ward frown a little before he smoothed over his features and told me,

"He will be fine, Little Carino, but it is time to get you out of here." It was at this that I finally looked around to see us situated on a slight hill, overlooking the burning compound of warehouses and buildings that looked like Hell had taken over it. We had parked at the side of the quiet road, and I was sitting facing Ward in a large SUV while he was standing outside with the passenger door open.

"The girls, did they...?" I closed my eyes, unable to finish that question.

"Hey, calm for me now. The girls were all saved," Ward told me, and I looked up into his perfect amber eyes, a pair that swirled with so much emotion, I could see now what this night had taken from him. He looked so relieved and before that emotion, I knew first came the intense worry.

"And Gomez?" At this, his jaw hardened for a second.

"Dead, and now burning like the rest of his kingdom as it falls," he said, looking back over at the same destruction I could now see. I nodded at this and reached up to cup his face. Then I told him softly,

"Then we won." At this he put his forehead to mine, something I knew he did when his emotions were at the point of need to express them.

"I am so fucking proud of you," he told me ardently.

"Of me?" I questioned, surprised by his statement.

"You were so brave, Eden, *so fucking brave,"* he said, making me melt against him, clinging on for as long as I could. Then he pulled back a little and told me,

"It's time to go."

"Where are we going?" I asked, making him nod to Deke who looked to have been making sure we weren't followed. Then he communicated something silently to his friend before he took a seat behind the wheel, closing the driver's door. Ward was letting me go when I told him quickly,

"I can scoot over." Then I did, so he wouldn't have to walk all the way round. This made him chuckle, and I had to say that after what we had been through, it was just like one of his warm hugs...

Comforting.

After this we drove into the city, and considering I had been blindfolded on the way here, now I was looking up out the window as if I was some wide-eyed puppy with a wagging tail. Ward's chuckle brought me back to the fact he was staring at me. So, I told him,

"I've never been to New York before, it's like being in a giant movie set." Ward laughed before pulling me to him, and soon I was transported back to only days ago when he had been the one to kidnap me. He picked me up and placed me on his lap, meaning I had no choice but to open my legs and sit astride him.

"There is only one sight I relish to see," he told me, making me grin in one of those loved up sappy ways, but yet I still teased,

"Is it a burger with everything on it, but anchovies?" At this he threw his head back and burst out laughing, something that made me shake as I was sitting on him. Then, without teasing me back, he got the hint and pressed a button so he could communicate to Deke,

"Food first, Deke, my Siren is hungry." I grinned at this and replied,

"That she is." Then I pulled his hand off the button and growled over his lips...

"Hungry for her Enforcer."

CHAPTER 17
'YOU SEXY THING'

As much as I wanted to continue kissing Ward, I was in fact starving. So, as a man of his word, he had Deke pull up outside a fast-food place so I could get a burger. One that tasted like heaven, which was why I couldn't help but moan as I ate.

"That is not helping," Ward grumbled, making me laugh.

"What isn't?" I asked innocently.

"You know precisely what you are doing," he countered, making me tease,

"Who, me?" Then I purposely took a big bite and moaned louder. He groaned this time, making me giggle. I continued eating on my side of the seat, as eating in his lap would have just been awkward and mean, especially with the way I continued to tease him. However, the second I finished and was just putting down my soda, I cried out in surprise as he plucked me from my seat and placed me back in his lap.

"Finally," he whispered into my neck, making me grin, as I loved that he couldn't wait to get me back into his arms. After this moment, things got heavy and heated between us pretty

quickly, as kissing Ward always did. But then he pulled back a little and buried his head in my neck, chuckling.

"What is it?"

"Deke just asked me if I wanted him to leave while I claim you in the car." I looked around and it became clear that neither of us had realized until now that he had parked, as we had arrived at our destination. At this I burst out laughing and threw my arms around him, hugging him to me.

"It's okay, Deke, we are behaving now!" I shouted so he would hear, making Ward growl before biting my neck playfully, telling me,

"You might, but I never will, not with you in my life."

"Okay, but can I at least get out of this dirty dress and shower first?" I replied, making him chuckle.

"Only if I can hold the soap," was his witty response, making me whisper in his ear,

"You're on, Hero." After this we were back to kissing and this time, I was the one who couldn't wait. Making me tell him over his lips in between kisses,

"Tell him I've changed my mind… *let's stay and misbehave together."* At this he pulled back, and his eyes flashed darker before my hair was in his fist and he was keeping me captured to his kiss. I briefly heard the sound of a car door slamming, which was cue enough for me to act. I quickly tried to fumble for his pants, lifting myself up on my knees enough to snake my hand down in there. We both moaned when I took hold of his very hard erection. Then I lifted myself up and told him between kisses,

"Tear… my… panties…off." He growled at this and shredded the sides, and they fell away a single second before I was lowering myself down on him, crying out in pleasure when he filled me. It was like coming home.

"Fuck me, so Gods be damned perfect!" Ward told me,

making me moan again, both at what his words did to me and what his body continued to do. He framed my hips with his large hands and continued to guide me, although I could tell he was struggling with his need by going at my slower pace. But then came what he had been waiting for. This was confirmed when shortly after I cried out my orgasm, he growled,

"I need more... always need more of you... I want fucking all of you!" Then I was suddenly flipped to being beneath him, and after dragging my ass to the edge of the seat, he reared back up inside of me, deeper than before. I cried out at the pleasure of it, arching my back as he powered into me. He held a hand to the back of the seat to steady himself as his other arm banded around my back to keep me up at the right level so he could get as deep inside me as possible.

His strength and stamina were incredible and I was soon coming yet again, screaming out my pleasure which felt even louder in the small space. I had nothing left to do than just hang on to his jacket, glad it wasn't bare skin, or I might have shredded him with my nails. Not that he would have minded, but I would have felt guilty all the same.

I didn't know how long we were at it but my third orgasm had just erupted out of me when I felt him tense as my channel was fluttering around his cock. Then, just as I was about to ask if anything was wrong, he suddenly roared out his own release, surprising both of us.

"Fuck! AHHH!" He continued to shout as he emptied himself into me, finishing this intense feeling when he placed his forehead to the back of the seat, giving me more of his weight and cocooning me with the whole of his body. I started stroking his neck as he panted through the pleasure that clung to him, making him shiver at my touch.

"You okay, baby?" I asked softly, and he pulled back so he could look at me.

"I am now I have you back," he said softly before kissing my forehead and making me melt against him.

Everything was perfect.

✿

"Seriously, are you thinking of starting a collection?" I said the moment I watched him pocket my panties and his reply had me howling with a fit of laughter.

"I'm thinking of creating a shrine to them in my basement."

"I don't want to know what's in your basement," was my comeback as we made our way across the underground parking to what I gathered was one of the many skyscrapers in New York.

I had kind of been busy toward the end of the drive, I thought grinning to myself.

"You will soon find out, when I finally get you home," he said, typing in some code to the elevators.

"Home?" I questioned as I started breathing quicker at the idea of it. At this Ward tensed, no doubt now believing the battle wasn't over.

"Eden, we have discussed this, and I understand this is all fast for you, but I will not bend on this... *I am* taking you home," he told me as the door opened, taking my hand in his and as he was about to pull me through, I held back.

"I haven't had a home for a long time... not a real one... not since... she was still alive." I added this last part painfully, making him swallow hard.

"Eden, my Little Carino," he said softly, but before he could say more, my head snapped up and I asked with excitement,

"Can we have a Christmas?" At this his eyes softened

126

further, as a tenderness came over them. Then he lowered his head and shook it a little, whispering to himself,

"You're killing me here." Then before I could even track his movements, I was grabbed quickly, and spun up against the wall, then he tipped my head back with a hold on my chin.

"I will give you the world if you ask me to." Then he kissed me and this time instead of it being a sexual fever, it was a slow burn that spoke only of the love this man had for me.

Needless to say, I melted into him and the ding of the doors opening wasn't even enough to get me to stop kissing and clinging onto this man. No, all it did was let us know that we were no longer alone. Something made obvious when we both heard the sound of someone clearing their throat.

"I think this is our cue to exit the elevator and find a room… or broom closet," I said, making him chuckle.

"I would say a dirty alleyway, but it doesn't look like that type of joint… more swanky," I added, and he grinned down at me, before reminding me,

"And not many alleyways on the 53rd floor."

"That's true, plus we already did it in the car," I reminded him, making him chuckle again.

"Gods, Ward, do me a favor and go ravish your Siren before all my men need to take a break just to jerk one off," Hel said, coming around the corner with a smirk on his handsome face. I chuckled at this, especially when Ward's arms tightened around me, followed by a growl.

"Oh, ease up, he wasn't talking about with me on their minds." Ward narrowed his eyes at me, and Hel just winked, telling me I was wrong.

"Oh… Ohh! Okay yeah, let's go get a room then," I said, only realizing the truth on the second 'oh' I made, one that sounded more prominent than the first. Hel started laughing before telling Ward,

"Go take care of your woman, our meeting can wait." Ward nodded before taking my hand once more and leading me from the elevator, making me blush when I saw for myself just how many of Hel's men were stationed in the lobby.

Ward pulled me along the opposite side of what seemed like an entrance to a nightclub, as you could hear the heavy beat thundering out of speakers. But because I wanted to lighten the tension of all the men now looking, well, uncomfortably turned on, I shouted back,

"Now remember, lads, lotion makes for a smoother motion!" At this Hel threw his head back and laughed. But as for Ward, he just groaned before swinging me around so he could sweep my feet from under me.

"Too much?" I asked, making him pretend to bite me as I giggled the rest of the way. I also knew which door it was from a hallway of many, as Deke was standing outside one ready to be on guard. He was also chuckling.

"You're off duty tonight, Deke, so go fucking relax and have a beer on me."

"I will need a fucking case of whiskey on you after tonight," he replied, making me laugh.

"Then you have some drinking to do, my friend," Ward said, putting a hand to his shoulder before opening the door to what I gathered was a spare room.

"Does everything with you guys have to come with so much fucking...? I mean the word!" I said, making Ward growl playfully at me.

"Yes, and soon to be the meaning of it," Ward declared boldly as he led me in there before him and just before the door closed, Deke winked at me and said,

"And that, as usual, is my cue to leave... Oh, and thanks for the tip, Eden." Informing me the reason for his chuckling was that he had heard my comment made to Hel's men. This meant that by the time Ward closed the door, he was shaking his head at the memory, most likely asking what he was going to do with me. Well, I knew exactly what he could do with me…

Round two in the shower anyone? Hehe.

"You do know that I can still read your thoughts… right?" Ward asked, reminding me. So, to get my own back, I just thought of his hot body wearing a pink tutu as he danced to 'You sexy thing' by Hot Chocolate. At this he started choking and coughing as I walked through the room I barely took notice of. Then I started to strip off my barely survived dress and walked boldly into the bathroom while swaying my hips.

The problem with this, I totally messed up my sexy statement by walking into a closet instead. Of course, this didn't matter to Ward, as the animalistic growl was my only warning before he acted. Although, he did find me turning around and shamefully trying to explain,

"Erm, I'm actually looking for the bathroom… whoa!"

"Tough shit, you found me instead!" he said, before picking me up and throwing me over his shoulder wearing nothing but my bra. Then he turned and headed for what I presumed was the right direction to the bathroom, as well… he passed the bed.

It looked as if he was going to hold the soap after all.

Although, how clean he was hoping to get me was anyone's guess, especially for the next hour, all I did was bombard him with…

My dirty thoughts.

CHAPTER 18

TROUBLE
WARD

I held Eden until I was assured she was out for the count. This was admittedly after wearing her out when she most likely needed anything but rest after what she had been through these past few days. But then I couldn't help it, as just one look at the girl and I was lost. However, it was also clear this wasn't one sided as she knew exactly what she was doing taking off her dress like that. And just walking into the closet was too fucking cute, had she not been naked, I would have teased her a little before just throwing her over my shoulder like a fucking caveman!

I was like a man obsessed... no, not like, *I fucking was a man obsessed!* My biggest nightmare had played out when I thought I had lost her. The moment I saw that helicopter crash into the building she was in, I swear I lost my fucking mind. Every single fiber in my body wanted me to drop to my knees and beg the Gods with my own life as payment for them to ensure her safety. Yet in this instant, my Darkness acted first, flying down to the wreckage, getting there just as the fucking thing blew!

Again, I would have fallen to my knees and begged had it

not been for my Darkness, who would not let me fall. So, with a roar of anger, I flew around the building, looking for another way inside, with my biggest fears playing out…

My girl was trapped inside.

I found another loading bay on the other side and dropped to the ground like a fucking thunderbolt. I was about to destroy the doors when gunshot fired, stopping me dead. However, as soon as the doors rolled up, I knew this had been just a quicker way to blow out the lock from a distance as they opened up to reveal Hel's men running out, all carrying an unconscious woman. I looked to Wrath's second in command, a man named Boaz, who simply nodded his head, telling me silently all I needed to know…

They had found my Eden.

The relief I felt was indescribable, and my Darkness had evaporated instantly, allowing me and my mortal vessel to take control once more. Our Siren was safe. It was all that mattered, that and getting her back into my arms as soon as possible. Something that happened the moment Wrath was seen running toward me with her unconscious form in his hold.

"She inhaled some smoke after the blast and is in need of healing," he told me in a stern but quiet tone, as I could see how hard he must have fought to save her. I took her in my arms and it was only then that I finally felt myself able to breathe.

"I am forever in your debt, Kaiden Wrath." At this he slapped a large hand to my back and told me,

"A bottle of The Balvenie and we will call it even." I grinned at that, telling him,

"I could buy you the whole fucking distillery and it wouldn't be enough." At this, Wrath scoffed and watched as the women his men carried out were being put safely in vehicles.

"Are there any more?" I asked, making Wrath shake his

head, one covered in dirt and ash. However, seconds after I said this, a woman's scream was heard.

"Fuck!" Wrath hissed, looking back and seeing the flames now getting closer to the offices at the side that must have been where one of the girls was taken. *Where one of the girls had been missed.*

"Brother, we have to leave, the place is gonna fucking blow!" Hel said after removing his tactical helmet as he approached us both.

"He's right, Kai, she is lost," I agreed, especially after seeing now there was very little chance of any of us getting to the poor girl in time. However, Wrath clearly didn't agree, and he growled his response at the same time snatching his brother's helmet from him.

"Not if I can help it... now go, get back to the club and I will meet you there!"

"But I am not leaving you..." his brother tried, grabbing his arm and trying to prevent what he no doubt believed to be madness.

"You will do as I fucking order you to do, little brother, now go and get these women out of here!" Wrath growled back, making his decision known before he turned to me and shocked me with his honest words.

"Take your Siren, while I make sure there are none left in there so no other Enforcer feels the same pain of losing one as you might have this night... GO!" After this he put the helmet on and started running back inside, despite my fears of what he would find once he got in there... disappointment or failure.

However, the strangest feeling came over me, while those on Wrath's council were trying to prevent Hel from running in there after him. Especially when parts of the building started to explode, making me protect my Siren, by moving closer to where Deke was bringing one of the SUV's closer. This feeling was as if we were being watched by something unseen. A presence that was as confused as it was hurt by what was being witnessed.

A single female voice somewhere in the world was screaming…

No.

After this, Hel was convinced to do as his brother had ordered and as for me, I had my Siren to heal. Something I had done the moment I felt we were far enough away from the site, one that was now primarily consumed by the flames that had spread. My wish to see Gomez's world burning had finally come to fruition, my only regret was that he died too quickly and before he had chance to see his world crumbling for himself.

But watching as one building after another started to fall, I could only hope that my friend had found the girl and got out of there before the worst had happened.

Hence my concern when discovering that Wrath still hadn't returned. It was also something Hel conveyed to me silently as I knew the knowledge would upset Eden. Something she didn't need right now as she had been put through the emotional ringer and I wasn't keen to add to it. Which was why I forced myself to leave her side, so I could get this meeting between Hel and myself out of the way before I made plans to leave.

Because I knew now that the amulet changed things. My plans to take Eden to the place I called home were going to have to wait as I was still an Enforcer, and I had a job to do. Which was why I slipped from between the sheets after kissing my Siren on her bare shoulder, before covering her naked form. Gods, she was so beautiful it was almost painful. I swear I would feel this ache in my chest, like never before, every time I looked at her. Like now, it was actually painful leaving her, yet I knew this place was a Gods be damned fortress in the sky and there was no chance at anything hurting her here.

Despite this knowledge, I still changed quickly, eager to get this meeting over with so I could get my girl on a flight out of here. I knew that Gomez was dead, but with this amulet near burning a fucking hole in my pocket the entire way here, I knew my problems were far from over, and that included the possible threat.

Besides, this wasn't my sector to rule and despite how much I liked and respected the Wrath brothers, I still would only feel easy when back in my own kingdom. Just like any Enforcer would, especially when being lucky enough to find their Siren the way I had.

I strode from the spare apartment, one of many that was kept for guests. Even the King had been known to stay here a time or two, just like he did at a few of my own homes throughout the ages.

I locked the door with a thought and now wearing the spare clothes that had been left for me by fuck only knows who, I walked down the hallway. I hated not wearing my own clothes but seeing as mine were stained by my recent kills, I didn't think it wise to do anything but burn them at this point. Thankfully, they had been black as I doubt making love to Eden in the car would have happened if I had looked like I bathed in blood splatter.

At least my Darkness had kept most of the gore from my mortal vessel but still, it didn't make for the sexiest of looks. So, with that in mind, I sent silent thanks to whoever had been responsible for me walking into the brothers' club wearing a plain black tee, jeans and heavy biker style boots that had too many leather straps if you asked me. But then beggars couldn't be choosers, and I was thankful that they had also provided Eden with a set of clothes. I had burned that dress, right along with my own clothes, wanting no memory of this night for as long as I fucking lived! Although, I had saved her panties and the amulet from my fury before destroying them.

Once again, I found myself walking into 53 Sins, and being welcomed the moment I did. I had already instructed Deke to speak with Hel on my behalf, telling him of the amulet and keeping him updated of my beliefs of what it could be. As for now, Deke was sitting at the bar and as soon as he saw me nod at him, he knew he was back on guard duty, despite my earlier statement. He was also a full bottle of whisky down and had half left of his second. Not that this would affect him, as alcohol rarely did, unless it came straight from the source of Hell or Heaven, of course.

But it was enough to help us relax as the very most. Which was why, as he passed me, I took the half bottle he offered and took a long and much needed swig. Then I took a seat in the place that was ready for me.

"Now that is the look of a relieved man," Hel commented, making me release a sigh before rubbing a hand down my face and commenting,

"Fuck yeah." Then as he raised his own bottle to me and I did the same when he said,

"Then we will drink to the fucking wins!" I nodded before partaking in his toast.

"I fear such a debt owed to you both will never be paid, for the weight of it is unsurmountable."

"I have a feeling that there will come a time when all fated Enforcers will have to unite, but until that day comes, don't mention it," Hel said, tipping the head of his bottle to me again before drinking it back.

"I was hoping to thank your brother, but I take it he is not back yet?" At this Hel visibly gritted his teeth and told me,

"No word as of yet."

"I am at your disposal if you need me," I informed him.

"If what you told me is true, then I would say you have bigger tasks on your hands, but I thank you all the same. No, my brother will return, I am sure of it," Hel said as he could no doubt still feel the link between them, keeping his hope alive. But then what could have befallen him I had no idea, because if the burning pits of Hell couldn't touch him, I doubt a burning building could.

"It is true, for why that fuck stain would have this amulet on him is beyond my comprehension," I admitted with a frustrated sigh.

"Perhaps he obtained it for a reason?" Hel asked, raising a brow in that cunning and knowing way of his, telling me he was well aware there was something I wasn't telling him. But then, there weren't many Enforcers out there that would admit to the discovery of a weakness.

"Perhaps," I replied without giving anything away, and yet Hel made it look as if I had said everything. I swigged back my whisky, knowing of the brothers' collection, sharing the same love for the amber liquid.

"I was hoping you could shed some light on where he might have bought it from... you still have that tech guy under your employ?" I asked.

"Franklin... yeah, if anyone can dig it up, it's him." He pulled his phone from his pocket and rang Franklin, telling him what I wanted. Then he hung up to let him see what he could find, if anything. Fuck, but for all I know, he could have received the fucking thing in the mail with a note saying to use on scary supernatural fuckers that want to rip your intestines out before kicking you off a fucking roof. Damn, but I had killed that fucker too quickly! A hundred goes at it would have been too quick!

"There is something you should know," Hel said gaining my attention. I raised a questioning brow before he told me,

"When we did a sweep of the building your girl had been kept in, we found a body."

"We left many, what of it?" I asked dryly.

"The ID on him said his name was Jimmy... name ring any bells?"

"Fuck! It's Eden's brother," I hissed, knowing she was going to be fucking devastated, despite being glad of it myself. Especially considering I had intended on getting my revenge, even if it hadn't been taking the fucker's life like I would have wanted.

"Yeah, that's what I thought... can't imagine watching her own brother getting his head shot to shit wasn't a mind fuck," Hel said, making me sit up as every muscle tensed.

"What did you say?" I asked in a cold tone.

"She didn't tell you?" he asked instead.

"No, but how do you know this?" Hel released an awkward sigh as it was clear he got no pleasure from this. I could tell that in his tone when he informed me,

"Her scent was in the same room on the chair opposite, one as fresh as his. Trust me, she was in that fucking room."

"Fuck!" I hissed again when hearing this, hoping, no near fucking praying, that it wasn't true. That Eden hadn't been forced to witness that. I hadn't even heard it in her thoughts... no, he must have been wrong. She would have told me.

Wouldn't she?

"Brave girl," Hel commented as if to himself, drinking back another swig, making me near growl. Because I knew why he had said that, knowing now that if it was true, then she obviously hadn't told me. She had just experienced it and instead of dwelling on it, she had focused on surviving. She had concentrated on saving others and not coming out of there

138

hysterical, despite having to witness all the carnage she had. Fuck, but the death of her own brother would have been enough to do it, and I wouldn't have fucking blamed her for even a second of it... *how could I?*

But yet again, she had astounded me with her bravery and force of will. She was most definitely a survivor and because of that strength, she had also saved seven other lives, who no doubt would never know who they had to thank. Luckily, Hel's phone rang and saved me from having to comment, as I wasn't ready to face the reasons why she hadn't told me.

"You're fucking shitting me? Email me the details!" Hel ordered before hanging up.

"What is it?" I asked impatiently. However, he looked down at his cell for a few seconds, obviously waiting for the email before he tossed me the phone.

"Take a look for yourself, recognize anyone we know," he said, and it took me all of two seconds to hone in on the name he was referring to, making me snarl.

"Gastian!"

"Yeah, and the Lega Nera. Now why doesn't hearing these fuckers are working together surprise me?" Hel gritted out, as this underground black market action house had been the bane of most Enforcers' existence.

"He fucking knew!" I snarled again, referring to Gomez.

"Knew what?" The sound of her voice behind me had me sucking in a breath, how the fuck had she done that without me knowing she was there?! She had unknowingly masked herself from me and I swear it was just one more reason to grit my teeth.

"You should be in bed!" I snapped, hating myself the second I did it. But instead of feeling the sting of my reprimand, she simply walked over to me and put herself in my lap, telling me,

"Now why would I do that when you were no longer in it with me?" Then bold as brass, she winked at me and shook my nose. I swear if she had been anyone else, just touching my nose like that would have been enough to get their soul collected. But as it was, I swear my fucking Darkness purred at this and if it'd had a fucking tail, it would have been wagging the fuck out of it right now!

"Now back to who knew what?" she asked again, this time looking at Hel and snuggling her ass even further into my dick. Gods, but did she even know what she was doing or was the innocent act just that... *an act?* Half of me hoped it was, so I had the excuse to punish her ass. The other half wanted me to keep her innocent, as it was a fucking turn on and I wasn't even ashamed to admit it.

"Looks like Gomez was stepping outside of his mortal parameters," Hel replied, surprising me by being so open. Eden looked back at me over her shoulder at this. The wide-neck cream sweater she wore, fell off one side, making me rub my chin against it before kissing her there.

"It is nothing to worry about," I told her, and I wasn't lying... *she had nothing to worry about.* I, on the other hand, did.

"So let me get this straight, Gomez was working with one of the good guys?"

"No." I growled but again she didn't even flinch at the sound of my anger, which I took as a gift, now knowing that she was getting used to me and trusted me never to harm her, even in my anger.

"But this person, is another Enforcer... yes?" she asked, linking the gaps.

"Not all Enforcers are as honorable as us, sweetheart," Hel replied with a wink that made me snarl at him.

"Ward!" she reprimanded but it didn't matter, as I still

glared at the cocky fucker, and he knew it with that fucking grin of his.

"We are a possessive lot, get used to it, Eden, he will not likely change and nor should he, as there are few that would," Hel replied, making me scoff my acceptance in that statement, as I had been ready to rip the fucker's head off and he was someone I considered a friend.

"So, this Enforcer... do you think he could have been the other person trying to pay Gomez for me?" At this I went rock solid beneath her and for once, it had nothing to do with having her ass sitting on my dick.

"What did you say?"

"Oh dear, little Siren..." Hel paused before saluting the tip of his bottle in her direction, finished with an understatement of the fucking year...

"...You're in trouble now."

CHAPTER 19
FLIGHTY RESPONSE
EDEN

I had to say, I was starting to think there were more important things that should have come before having sex twice with Ward, despite how it was the obvious and preferred choice. I knew this the moment he put his hands under me and stood with me in his arms.

"Inform me if your brother returns," Ward said, making me gasp, as I looked around to realize that my big Viking looking savior wasn't here with his brother. A person I had hoped to have been given the opportunity to grant my thanks.

"Where is he?" I asked but Ward growled at me,

"It is not wise to ask after another man right now, for I am on the edge as it is," he replied, clenching his jaw, and I frowned at this before snapping,

"Are you serious? I am not allowed to ask about the guy who walked through fire to get me!?" His face said it all, making me respond,

"Unbelievable."

Once again, we soon found ourselves back in the room where he put me on the bed, dropping me after growling,

"Believe it."

"Hey!" I complained as he walked away, and I had to say the sheets were still warm, that was how little time it had been when waking up and finding myself alone.

"Ward, what exactly is your problem?" I asked in exasperation, making him sigh before dragging a hand through his hair in what looked like frustration and telling me truthfully,

"It should have been me, okay!"

"What?" I asked in shock.

"Who saved you, it should have been me!" he shouted again, making me flinch. Not because he was angry but because of the pain heard in his words. This was when I got up on my knees and made my way to the edge of the bed.

"Ward, please come here." He released another sigh before taking the few steps needed to make it back to me. Then I raised my hands up to frame his handsome face, watching as he closed his eyes and sighed at the contact. I had to say that it warmed my heart to know the affect I had on him. The affect I had on this hard and scary man who became putty in my hands.

"Hard as a fucking rock more like," he muttered dryly, reading my thoughts and making me bite my lip to stop myself from grinning. Instead, I released my own sigh and told him,

"There is only one hero in my life, and he is the Angel I look at now. The one who saved me far more than I ever even knew that I needing saving." He opened his eyes at this and whispered my name,

"Eden."

"I was living a lie, Ward, making myself believe I was happy." He cupped the back of my neck and gave me a squeeze before saying,

"Sweetheart."

"It's true, I was just living through the motions, never really allowing myself to get close to anyone again. After my mom died, I was taken from my whole world. Jimmy and his dad were all I had but one by one even they left me, both of them choosing crime over the love I had tried to give them. I was... *always alone.*" I shuddered through this last part, finally allowing the tears to fall, causing him to pull me into him and hold me like no one had done for so long.

"You will never be alone again... do you understand, Eden... I will never leave you, not even in death, for I would fight my way back to you... *I would fight the world for you.*" On hearing this vow, I broke down and sobbed, clinging onto him now as if the possibility of his words were nothing but a dream.

The most perfect dream there ever was.

֎

"Erm... I am not sure I can even do this," I said as we pulled up next to what was obviously a private jet, now getting nervous and making Ward chuckle as I took in the plane for the first time. Deke opened his door, making me jump, something Ward tried to hide his grin at before exiting the car. Then he turned to give me his hand, telling me,

"You will be fine, my Little Carino." I looked at his hand and then back at the plane I had never really believed I would ever go on. However, I must have been taking too long in trusting him as he flexed his fingers and told me more sternly,

"Now give me your hand, Eden." I swallowed hard, knowing there was no way I could get out of this, other than do as he asked, meaning I gave him what he wanted. I then let him pull me from the car, chuckling when he saw my face of dread. He pulled me into him and tipped my chin back so he could have my eyes when he asked,

"Do you trust me?"

"I don't have a passport," I replied softly, making him fight his grin.

"It's been taken care of, now answer my question, do you trust me?"

"I don't have anything to wear for a hot country... I don't actually have anything, period," I replied, and again I got a lip twitch as he fought another grin. Then he tried to act more serious and with a growl of words, told me,

"You trust me." Then he tossed me over his shoulder, making me cry out in shock. Deke just chuckled as he watched Ward forcefully carry me on board.

"Ward!" I shouted his name before demanding in my most stern voice,

"Warden Za'afiel, put me down right this second or so help..." I paused the moment he did as I demanded, and I was upright once more. Meaning the rest of my words came out weak as he was now towering over me, walking me backwards.

"Erm... me." I finished my sentence, making him fight another knowing smirk as he continued to herd me to where he wanted me. Meaning I wasn't exactly shocked when the backs of my legs felt one of the seats behind me before I fell back into it. Then he placed a hand at the headrest and leaned in so there were only intimidating inches between us.

"You... Miss Eden Teles... don't have to worry about a thing," he told me, after first emphasizing my name as I had done to his, and then he kissed me quickly before taking the opulent seat next to me. It looked more like a luxury apartment than the inside of a plane as obviously I had never seen anything like it before. It was all cream leather and gleaming polished wood, with what looked like freshly laid carpets that were thick enough you could sink your toes into. Even the seats looked like the most expensive lazy boys you could have bought and were quite possibly the most comfortable seats I had ever sat in.

Yet all of this was quickly overshadowed by my fear of the unknown.

"You do remember the part when I told you I have never been on a plane... right?" I reminded him, making him grin at me, before taking my hand to raise to his lips for a kiss.

"You will be fine," he told me gently and kept my hand firmly in his.

"How can you be so sure, what if it starts to take off and the engines fail... wait, how are the brakes on this thing... does it get regular maintenance, oil changes, new wheels, things like that?" At this he burst out laughing, literally needing to put a hand to his belly as he roared with hilarity. I yanked my hand from his, telling him sarcastically,

"I'm glad my anxiety amuses you!" At this he released a sigh, letting go of his amusement long enough so he could turn in his seat to face me.

"Look at me." I huffed at this and crossed my arms over my cream sweater, that belonged to God only knows who.

"Eden, sweetheart, grant me your pretty eyes." I couldn't deny him, especially not in that soft, tender voice of his. So, naturally, I looked at him.

"I am sorry if my reaction offended you, but I will not apologize for finding your reactions a delight," I huffed again, making him grin.

"Now as for your fear, there is simply no need for it."

"No? Aircraft mechanic in your spare time, are you?" I snapped back, but it didn't do anything to remove his smirk. Then he pulled me close, tugging on my sweater so he could whisper in my ear,

"No, but I do have wings, sweetheart." I released a heavy sigh at this and before I could say anything, he took my hand once more and kissed the back of it, telling me,

"Now relax."

"Easy for you to say, Wing Man," I muttered, making him chuckle again. After this, I was left to listen to all the strange noises a plane must make before take-off, jumping even after the stewardess had closed the door.

"What's wrong with her?" Deke asked when taking his own seat, relaxing back as though he had done this a million times and well, he most likely had.

"She... has never been on a plane before," I answered for myself making Deke grin.

"Statistically, it's safer than driving," he informed me, making me narrow my gaze at him.

"Yes well, I'm sure those same statistics say it's safer being on a rollercoaster than being in a car, but I don't like those either, so being trapped in a metal cylinder with wings..."

"And engines... don't forget the engines, Edie," Deke added quickly.

"Oh yes, not forgetting the things that require fuel and therefore can easily blow up on landing," I added, making them both chuckle, something I ignored.

"Anyway, where I was I?"

"I believe you were up to a metal cylinder with wings," Ward replied smoothly, no doubt trying to hold back another grin.

"Like I was saying... oh shit! What was that?" I shouted, grabbing onto Ward as if he was my own personal lifejacket, making me quickly ask,

"Does this plane have those air baggy things that pop down when we need oxygen?" Then I quickly started to fumble with my seatbelt, unable to get it clicked with my shaking hands. At this Ward released a sigh and nodded toward Deke, obviously silently giving him an order to give us privacy. I only knew this as he got up out of his seat muttering,

"Good luck." I of course took this the wrong way, shouting,

"Good luck?! Why did he say that, why would we need luck?!" At this, Ward brushed aside my hands and made me scream as he plucked me out of my seat and placed me on his lap. I started squirming, telling him,

"We need to be in our seats... oh God, it's moving!" I shouted, making him tighten his arms around me and tell me,

"Calm for me now, Eden, or you will force me to take matters into my own hands." I let his words sink in, causing my eyes to widen before I looked up at him.

"What does that mean?" Again, he sighed at this.

"It means doing what I did when you ran from me," he replied in a tense tone. My eyes shot frantically to the front of the plane as we started to pick up speed, and then quickly to the window to see water streaming across it until we were going so fast it disappeared! This made me shout,

"Do it!"

"Eden."

"I mean it, Ward, make me pass out, sleep for a week, dream of fucking Carebears! I don't care just... just take away my fear," I begged, burying my head in his neck and clinging on, making me feel his sigh beneath me once more.

"Alright, sweetheart... alright," he whispered before tipping my face up to look at him, then he whispered over my lips,

"Sleep for me, my Angel... sleep and I will watch over you... I will protect you... I promise you this... sleep... sleep, Eden... Sleep, my Siren."

His voice lured me in and soon I felt myself looking into his dark eyes swirling with the power to draw me in and take hold.

Take hold of my dreams.

CHAPTER 20

HONEY, BABE AND ENFORCERS

T he next time I woke, I felt a gentle touch on my cheek and that same voice was luring me from my dreams. Dreams of golden sands and a turquoise ocean as far as the eye could see. I could even feel the comforting heat on my bare feet as I walked across the beach and this time, I didn't ask where my mother was…

I asked for Ward.

"Ward?"

"I am here, my Siren," his tender voice returned, and I felt my hair being stroked back, breaking the spell of my dream. Which was when I realized I was actually lying with my head in his lap. I yawned, making him chuckle softly before I started rubbing my eyes as I sat up to discover I was still on the plane.

"Oh wow, we didn't die after all," I commented, making him laugh this time, before pulling me into his side.

"As if I would allow such a thing," he told me, and I also realized he must have moved us both to one of the couches along the walls of the plane so I would be more comfortable.

"How do you feel?" he asked as I looked out at the window and was utterly amazed by the sight that met me. Which was

151

why I got out of my seat and got closer to the window. The same one he had once been sitting next to, before shooting a quick look back at him over my shoulder.

"We are in the clouds!" I exclaimed with a grin so big it would have made my cheeks ache. His soft smile in return was another sight that warmed my heart, as it was clear my astonishment was one that warmed his own.

"That we are, sweetheart," he replied in a tone that confirmed this.

"It's... God, but it's so beautiful," I said, placing my hand on the cool window as if I could reach out and touch them beneath us.

"That it is," he agreed in a tone that told me we weren't talking about the same thing. I blushed at this and smiled to myself before leaving the view in sight of a better one... *my Enforcer.* I casually walked over to him and sat down next to him, put my arms behind my head and joked,

"I knew this flying stuff would be a piece of cake." At this he burst out laughing, before pulling me to him so he could hold me. I giggled and kissed him, feeling no more fear, only my overwhelming love for him.

Shortly after this, I found myself sitting opposite him with a table between us so we could enjoy a meal together. I also found out that I had slept for about six hours, something he told me he thought I had needed.

"So, Spain, huh?" I asked, making him raise a brow at my not-so-subtle way of getting him to tell me why. Well, more of an explanation than I had received so far, which was one word... *Business.* But I had known instantly there was more to it than that, as the longer I was around Ward, the easier it was picking up on things. Like the way his jaw would harden if it was something he didn't want to talk about or was displeased when he had no choice to. The way his light brown eyes would change to a heated honey amber tone when I did something funny or something that turned him on. Admittedly, something that happened a lot and *something I liked a lot.*

"Oh, come on, you can't just be like... Spain, business... and then that's it," I said, mimicking his manly voice and making him give me a pointed look.

"Is that how I am perceived to speak?"

"Yes, Mr. I can melt the panties off a girl just by saying her name!" I replied, making him cough before laughing.

"Umm, I will have to try that," he commented, making me pick up a cherry tomato from my plate and throw it at him... but of course, he caught it... in his freaking teeth!

"Arggh, you're annoyingly smooth sometimes," I complained half-heartedly.

"Would you like to see me trip up sometime or perhaps I could amuse you with a fart?" At this I burst out laughing, thinking it was by far the funniest thing he had ever said!

"Oh my God, YES!" I replied, making him grin.

"Ask your question, love." he said instead, making me want to melt like ice cream when hearing him calling me 'love'.

"Why Spain, I thought you lived in Italy?"

"We live in Italy," he amended in a tone that told me he seriously believed this.

"No, you live in Italy, I am just your girlfriend tagging along for an extended visit," I amended, making him raise a single eyebrow,

"Extended visit? Is that what you are calling it?" he asked dryly.

"Don't freak me out here, Ward, yes, as your very new girlfriend, I am simply coming to stay with you," I informed him, granting him my own pointed look, one he ignored.

"You're not my girlfriend, Eden." At hearing this my heart sank a little but was given no time to drown there as he added,

"You are my woman, my Siren, my everything, and mine in every way possible. Meaning you may think of this as however you want, Eden, but the facts are simple, where I go, you go." As nice as this all sounded, it was also edged with an obsessive dominance that freaked me out a little. Okay, so more than a little, hence why I said,

"Okay, moving swiftly on... why Spain?" He gave me wry look at this but didn't comment. No, instead he pulled something wrapped in a red velvet cloth out of his pocket.

"Because of this," he said as he moved our plates to the side to make room.

"What is it?" I asked, unable to help whispering. He folded it back and revealed what looked an oversized ancient coin with a hole at one edge. I could only see one side, being too afraid to touch it to turn it over. But what I could make out was a bit of writing around the edge, that was in a language I couldn't detect, and three strange symbols in the center.

"A myth, or at least, it should have been," he replied in tense tone.

"Okay, you're going to have to give me more than that, honey," I said, and the look he gave me after calling him honey seemed like he was five seconds away from ravishing me.

"Focus, Ward," I added trying not to giggle.

"Then stop being cute and give me reason to focus, *baby,"* he said, replying in kind and making me turn mushy again.

"You're just trying to distract me so you can get lucky and become a member of the mile high club," I replied, making him scoff.

"Sweetheart, I consider myself more than lucky just sitting opposite you, and I don't need a damn plane to feel high when getting to fuck you." At this my mouth dropped before it closed and then it opened again ready to say something, but nothing came, so it closed again. This made him grin.

"Okay, you are seriously smooth... like, did you take an online course or something?" I finally found my intelligent voice, the one that knew all the best come backs. At this he just winked at me, and I pretended to fan myself, making him chuckle. Then, as a stewardess walked over to take our plates, Ward covered the coin thing, hiding it once more. This told me that it was something important enough not to risk people knowing about it. I also noticed the way he slipped it back into his pocket in an equally smooth motion.

She didn't seem to notice, instead focusing on her job and asking us if we wanted anything else, dessert or coffees, which we both declined. As for me, I was eager to continue our conversation.

"I know you must have a lot of questions, Eden."

"Ha, well that's the biggest understatement of the year!" I laughed and he gave me a sympathetic look in return.

"Alright, which one is it you want to know the most?"

"What's an Enforcer?"

"I am," he replied in short, and I had gathered as much, making me roll my hand around and prompt,

"And that is what exactly?" He released a sigh as if he knew all he was about to tell me was most likely one of the heaviest conversations we would ever have together.

"So, I think you have gathered by now the world you live in is not exactly the one you would have continued to believe it was, had you never met me of course."

"No shit," I commented dryly, making him grin.

"Angels and Demons, like myself and Wrath live among mortals, doing so for the most part, unseen and unknown to your kind," he told me.

"My kind?" I asked, needing him to elaborate.

"Human, sweetheart."

"Oh right, got ya... so how long have you been here?" I

asked then, and it felt odd, like I was asking him how long he had been living in a town or city, not how long he had been, well... *living for.*

"Our kind has been living in one way or another in this realm since the beginning of time, long before mortal men first walked it." My eyes widened at that, making me release a breath on a whoosh.

"Wow, okay... erm, so how have you stayed hidden so long?"

"Being able to manipulate minds helps, sweetheart," he said, making a good point.

"Ah, but of course," I commented, knowing this was still a sore spot with me. Which was most likely why he reached over the table between us and took my hand in his.

"I do not want some subservient mindless mortal by my side, Eden, for if I did, I would have taken one long ago... besides, it is forbidden for my kind to take a mortal." Now this information did shock me, as I let the gravity of his words really take hold.

"Take one where... oh wait, you're taking about to bed aren't you... shit!? But we did that! Oh no, does this mean you're going to be in trouble with like, your supernatural cops or something?" At this he started laughing, shaking his head a little before telling me,

"To begin with, Enforcers are like the cops of your world and secondly, I am allowed to take you wherever I want, and in whichever bed I want," he added with a growl of words before explaining,

"You may have gathered by now, but you are fated to be mine, Eden." I frowned at that and then horror struck.

"Does that mean that none of this is real!"

"No! Eden, no don't think like that, as all of this... it is very fucking real, trust me on that," he said, getting worked up at the very implications of my question.

"But you just said we were fated, what if I was someone else, what if I snored and drove you crazy or...?"

"You do snore, and I don't give a shit," he added, interrupting me.

"I do not!" I argued, even though yeah, I kind of did.

"Eden, you woke yourself up last night and asked me to be quiet as you were trying to sleep," he said, chuckling, naturally something I ignored.

"Yes, well my point is that I could have been anyone, Ward." At this he took both my hands this time and told me in earnest,

"But you're not just anyone, Eden, you are you and you're utterly perfect for me because you're you... do you understand?" I shook my head a little, telling him that I didn't.

"You were born to be mine, born to be..." he paused and then told me what I had been silently dreading him to say but needed him to explain all the same...

"My Siren."

CHAPTER 21
THE IMPORTANCE OF ANCIENT HISTORY

" *My Siren.* " I frowned before looking away, wishing and hoping that his words would take hold. I guess I just needed to let them.

"Why do you call me your Siren?" I asked this time and he let me go after first giving my hands a squeeze.

"That is what you are."

"And again, you're going to have to give me more than that," I told him, making him sigh.

"I understand that this is going to be a lot to take in and some of it, most likely hard to believe."

"Are you kidding?!" I shouted, startling him enough that he looked shocked.

"Ward, I just witnessed a battle involving Demons that controlled fire and Angels that had wings. Oh, and a magic dude, let's not forget the magic dude," I said, making him smirk.

"My point is, I think I am about as far past disbelieving as you can get." Hearing this made him nod in an accepting way and was enough to convince him to start telling me the story of Sirens. I had to admit, I felt sorry for them instantly and was a little shocked to hear just how callous some Gods could be. I had mentioned this to Ward, and he told me,

"Fuck, Eden, but you have no idea." I had a feeling that it was said with more personal venom, making me wonder if it had something to do with his own history and the reason why he was here and not up there. It wouldn't surprise me, considering sending those once in Heaven down to the mortal realm as he called it seemed to be common punishment for these Gods.

Even if there were actually innocent.

Like the Sirens.

"I have to be honest, this Zeus sounds like a right asshole," I whispered behind my hand, making Ward smirk.

"That's because he is," he replied in the same way, making me giggle. But then he went back to explaining how when the Sirens were punished and sent to Earth after being stripped of their powers, they were also protected by the Fates. Protected so they may one day produce a female offspring who will be destined to become a Siren once more.

"So, my mom... she...?" I tried to ask and Ward, seeing that I was struggling, took my hand and told me,

"No, Eden, she wasn't a Siren, she just came from a generation of those that carried the latent gene." I thought about this and then asked,

"But what if that's all I can do, how do we know I am an actual Siren." At this he chuckled softly and told me,

"Because you are Fated to find your Enforcer, your protector and guide, one that will tie you to him through love. I told you, the Gods may have wanted Sirens cursed but the Fates didn't, they wanted you protected and there is no better way than gifting you to one of the strongest of our kind." Ward's words, as confusing as they were, were also said in a comforting way... like an absolute.

"And you know I am yours because…?" I let that question linger there, making him release a sigh.

"I know this is hard for you to hear, but in my world, all any King or Enforcer wants is to be blessed enough by the Fates to be gifted a Chosen One and trust me when I say, they made it so that when it happens, *we fucking know about it."* He said this last part on a growl of passion, not one of anger. I also had to admit that his words certainly affected me, which was why I hugged him to me at that point.

"So just to clarify, you're sure I'm…"

"Yes, Eden, you are a Siren and more importantly, *you are my Siren,* there is no doubting either." I nodded, unable to find words after that one. Which is why he went on to tell me more about his world and mainly the pecking order of it.

"So, Afterlife and this Dominic Draven, who is he, like your boss or something?" I asked after hearing him mention him.

"Of a sorts. He is known as the King of Kings and rules over all our kind," Ward said, and I could tell with the way he said it, this was no doubt common knowledge in his world.

"King of Kings? Sounds like a poker champion." He laughed once, before telling me,

"He rules the world, but he is still only one being, which is where Enforcers come into play."

"Which you are?" I asked, wanting to be sure that I most definitely had that part right.

"Yes, the most powerful in fact," he replied, making my mouth drop.

"Come again?" I asked but he simply shrugged his shoulders and told me,

"I rule over the largest sector." Again, my reactions were all shock, making me press for more.

"Which is?"

"All of Europe." He said this like it was nothing and he was telling me he liked to play chess or something.

"All of Europe?!" My voice raised up a little at this, making him smirk.

"Yes," was his simple answer and for me, it was way too simple.

"As in… Europe?" I tried again, and his smirk turned into a full-blown grin.

"I only know of the one, sweetheart," he mocked gently, making me bite my lip.

"And you rule it?" Again, I was getting kind of stuck on this bit.

"I know this is a lot to take in, Eden, but you will come to understand our world in time." He sounded very confident when he said this.

"Ward, up until last week I was homeless, lived in my car and was surviving on noodles that I sometimes had to eat dry out of the packet because…"

"Don't fucking remind me, Eden," he growled, interrupting my tale of woe. So, I ignored this and continued.

"And now I find out my new boyfriend… oh, he only rules Europe, as in… all of it!" I said, getting loud and making him sigh, doing so no doubt at the sight of my dramatics.

"Oh, but that's not it, as for me, I am some Lost Siren fated to you, a descendent of some poor chick kicked out of Heaven by Zeus, who sounds like a right asshat by the way." I said this last part behind my hand again, as if he were actually here on the plane with us.

"I grant you, it's a lot to take in."

"Oh, you grant me, do you…? Thanks," I muttered sarcastically, making him give me a wry look.

"I am no fool, for I knew this was never going to be an easy conversation to have, Eden." I released a sigh at this, knowing I was being a bit of a bitch, so told him,

"I know, I am sorry, I am just trying to process this all, you know."

"You have nothing to be sorry for, my girl, although I do admit thinking it best to wait until getting you on a plane before telling you." I frowned in question, making him add with a gesture of his hand,

"Nowhere to run." I rolled my eyes at this, before asking him something he knew I really wanted to know.

"So, what's in Spain then?" At this he not only released a sigh, but he also palmed the back of his neck in what I knew was frustration.

"Being an Enforcer also comes with having your fair share of enemies."

"But of course, it does," I commented dryly, but then what could I say? I had no power and ruled over nothing but my car, although it ruled over me most of the time. But my point was, I was just a data analyst from North Carolina and still, I ended up with an enemy, so could I really be surprised that someone as powerful as Ward had a few? No, I couldn't.

"My current one is another Enforcer named Gastian."

"Another Enforcer? But I thought they were the good guys?" I asked, now getting even more confused.

"On the most part, we are, but there are some who get greedy with just their sector and want more. Wrath has been challenged before for his sector, as even though it is not the biggest, it is more powerful because of its cities and who it is closest to."

"And who is it closest to?" I asked before I could think about it, which was why Ward raised a brow and before I knew it, I was answering my own question.

"Afterlife."

"Yes, the King of King's heart of his rule, which means Wrath is favored by the King and that, in essence, means more power," Ward added, and I had to admit, I didn't think I would be spending half this journey learning supernatural politics.

"How about you?"

"Me?" He shook his head a little as if he didn't understand the question.

"Are you favored by the King?" I asked again because I was curious.

"Yes, I believe I am," he replied with a proud grin.

"Hence, the biggest sector," I added, making him chuckle once before he repeated,

"Hence the biggest sector."

"So this Gastian, I gather his sector is…"

"Very small," he finished for me, making me chuckle this time.

"Ah, so it's all about size." This made him laugh, especially when I wagged my little finger.

"It is small being that it was only Morocco, but this means our sectors are only separated by the Straits of Gibraltar," he said, making me add,

"So, what is that? Something like, nine miles of water?" I said, recalling this from memory but his look told me he was impressed.

"I was good in school, a bit of a geek actually and well, travelling has always been my dream so there is no need for you to look so surprised," I told him, making him smirk regardless.

"So, he wants Spain?" I guessed, making him ask,

"Why do you say that?" This question was a test as I could already tell he knew this already.

"It makes sense, considering that is where we are going now

and it's the closest country to him that's yours." He shrugged and then said,

"He wants Spain. The Caves of Nerja, to be precise."

"Caves? Why would he want…"

"These caves, they are a series of caverns close to the town of Nerja in the Province of Málaga. They stretch for almost five kilometers, so it is a little more than just a simple cave, mainly for what they hold within them," he said, interrupting my question with an in-depth answer.

"And what do they hold, the fountain of youth or something, the cure to little dick syndrome?" He laughed at this before surprising me with more.

"There is believed to be a hidden portal leading into the realm of Hell." At this my mouth literally dropped open.

"Erm… into Hell? As in the fiery pits of damnation…? That type of Hell?" He gave me a wry look and said,

"It's a little more than that but yes, we are talking about the same Hell."

"Wow, I wonder what the welcome committee is like there?" He chuckled at that before telling me,

"I can't be sure why he wants this access, but I believe it has something to do with the amulet I found, as he is working with an ancient group known as the Lega Nera."

"What is the Lega Nera?" I asked as he knew I would.

"It means Black League in Italian, where they founded their group, as black stands for the things they sell in their black-market trade. It started off as small as it could be, with one Demon vender selling whatever he could get his hands on from Hell and now, thousands of years later, it has become one of the biggest illegal auction houses in history." I let my breath go on a big whoosh of air once he had finished.

"So as an Enforcer…?" Again I let that question linger.

"It is my job to put a stop to it, although this is easier said than done," he admitted with a frustrated sigh.

"How come, too much red tape?" I asked, making him grin.

"No, not enough of it. The problem we face is that the auction house is always moving and doesn't give much time before it starts. Only members of the Lega Nera get warning of when it will arise and it could be anywhere in the world."

"You're right, that sound impossible."

"Oh, we will get them one day but as for Gastian, he is someone I intend to get far sooner," Ward said, making his eyes turn dark with deadly promise.

"So, he is involved, you say?"

"I believe he is," he agreed.

"In what way though?" I couldn't help but ask as really, I had a million questions about everything. But then I don't think anyone could really blame me for this.

"I think he is one of the vendors," Ward said, making me gasp before I then shouted,

"So that's what he wants with the caves!" Ward frowned a little before asking,

"Why do you say that?"

"Well, think about it, if what he really wants with part of your sector is the bit with a portal in it, then it makes sense if he sells stuff illegally, just think how much stuff he would have access to if he had his own portal and could pop in whenever he wanted to grab stuff to sell in this auction." At this my hand was grabbed and brought to his lips to kiss.

"Eden, you're a genius!" I giggled at this and blushed, feeling good that I could help.

"Well, I wouldn't go that far. I've just always enjoyed puzzles, that's all."

"I don't know why I didn't fully see it before, but now I do, it seems obvious," Ward admitted, making me tell him,

"Sometimes it's hard to see the wood for the trees, plus don't be too hard on yourself, you have been a bit preoccupied lately." I winked at him, making him smile at me.

"So does this also have anything to do with that amulet you found?" I asked, making him look toward the window, and I did the same to see that land was coming into view, giving me my first view of Spain. Then he looked back at me and said,

"I don't know but I think it's time…"

"An Enforcer finds out."

CHAPTER 22
AWOKEN FINGERS

"Who's that?" I asked the moment the plane landed and this time, Ward didn't need to put me to sleep as he found another way to distract me. Looking back, I knew this was what it had been after the stewardess had come to tell him something, only to be cut off with a shake of his head. Of course, I hadn't known this at the time, only later after he had positioned me in his lap once more and started kissing me, holding me tight, no doubt so I wouldn't feel the vibrations.

I had to say, the power of his kiss had to be honored here, as I would never have thought it possible to miss the plane landing. But the moment he had started chuckling, I knew I had indeed missed something big.

"What?" I had asked, making him reply on a playful growl,

"Best landing ever." This was when I finally realized we were back on the ground.

Which brought us to seconds after the plane had taxied to the right spot and the stewardess was now opening the door. This was also when I noticed that even though it was now getting dark, thanks to the well lit runway, I could see a man standing and waiting by another expensive looking car.

He was a tall, slim man who wore a light-gray suit that matched his salt and pepper hair. He also had a beaming grin that instantly put you at ease, seeing as you just knew that the guy would be a friendly type.

"That is Anders, and he works for me," Ward told me, making me grin before asking,

"In what way?" He raised a brow, and I couldn't help myself when saying,

"What? You have officially opened the Eden can of worms here... where from here on out, a million questions will come spilling from me." He laughed at this and pulled me in for a hug, before telling me,

"He is on my council and someone I trust, plus, he runs Spain for me," he added with a wink before letting me go and taking my hand, pulling me along as I muttered mockingly,

"Oh, he just runs Spain, no biggy." Ward yanked me hard to him and growled down teasing me,

"Behave, Siren." Then he pretended to bite me, making me giggle. After this, I let him lead me down the steps and I couldn't help but sigh in relief when feeling my feet touching the ground again. Of course, Ward noticed.

"It will get easier with time." I swallowed hard but didn't say anything. No, instead I continued to follow, seeing Deke who had somehow already made it off the plane without me even realizing it.

"My Lord, welcome back," the man said, bowing slightly and shocking the realization of all that Ward had told me in that one motion alone.

"Anders, my friend, it is good to see you again, although I wish it was under better circumstances," Ward replied, obviously referring to all he had told me on the plane.

"Yes, Gastian has gone too far for the King of Kings not to notice this time."

"Oh, he will notice alright, for that asshole's days are certainly numbered," Ward replied firmly.

"But I see you are not without good news, for I welcome you both," he said, bowing his head now to me and despite him being a friend Ward's natural instincts were to tuck me closer to his side.

"This is Eden, she is new to travelling long distances, so I am eager to get her into a comfortable bed to rest. It has been a long few days, my friend," Ward said, which I knew was a hint to get moving.

"But of course, everything is ready for you, and I secured you a room in Nerja, as you requested. It is only an hour's drive away."

"Where are we now?" I asked, making him grin.

"You are in the beautiful city of Malaga, my dear, however I am afraid much of it will be missed seeing as it is now dark... come, my Lord," Anders said, opening the door to the Limo which Ward guided me into with a possessive hand on my lower back. I lowered into the car and was quickly followed by Ward.

"Tired, am I?" I asked with a smirk. At this he pulled me closer, wrapping an arm around me and tucking me in under his arm, then he commented in a knowing tone,

"We shall see."

Ten minutes later, I was fast asleep.

⚜

The next time I awoke, I was surprised to find not only was I in another very comfortable bed with great sheets, but I was also the first to wake. I don't know why this surprised me, considering what Ward had been put through these last few days, but it did. I think it was because it was always happening the other way around, that it meant I had never really ever seen the guy sleep. I had woken up facing him, with his arm curled around my waist, making me lick my lips at the delicious muscles on show. But what my eyes settled on was the peaceful look on his face, making me want to reach out and touch him. To push back his tousled hair and run my fingers through it.

In truth, I was still getting used to touching Ward in that way, or at least being the first to do so, as it was different during sex. Touching each other was kind of a given. But when we were awake, I was cautious, and I didn't really know why. After all, he touched me constantly and like he… well, *like he owned me.* The thought made me want to squirm, as it was most definitely a turn on. But then if he owned me, then didn't that mean that he was also mine in return?

However, I didn't give in to my urges as I knew that he must have needed the sleep, being as he was obviously in a deep enough one that he didn't even stir when I shifted out of his hold on me. The room was filled with glorious sunshine, and I was eager to see outside. Which was why I slipped from beneath the sheets and padded my way to the bathroom, before completing morning business without flushing so as not to wake him. This also included quickly brushing my teeth, because hello, morning breath was anything but sexy. I was just thankful I found these things in the first place. Then I grabbed a robe, as Ward had clearly undressed me before putting me to bed.

As for the room, it was light and airy, with a Mediterranean feel, in its striped, blue sheets, its warm gray tones on the walls and its light wood furniture, that mimicked what I knew I would most likely find outside… its sandy beaches.

Speaking of which, I couldn't hold back any longer, as I

stepped toward the balcony. Unsurprisingly, I couldn't help but gasp as I took my first step through the glass doors. I had never seen anything like it, well, only in my dreams. I had never seen water so blue or so crystal clear, nor had I ever seen the sight of the ocean from so high up before. The balcony overlooked a private beach below and I couldn't help but smile at an old couple walking there. They were holding hands as if this was their favourite thing to do in the morning. I was so emersed in fact, that I shrieked in surprise when I felt a pair of arms circle me from behind.

"I have to say, sweetheart, not a fan of waking up to find you gone," he grumbled in my ear. His voice made husky from just waking.

"Technically, I am not gone as I am right here," I informed him, making him growl a little.

"You were not in bed, in my book that makes you gone from the place I want you," he said, biting my neck and making me moan, then I cried out surprised when he swept me up into his arms and walked me back inside.

"Now let's try this again, should we?" he mused with a bad boy grin before lowering me down and following by caging me in. Then he kissed me, and it was long and slow and sensual, so basically dreamy. Then he pulled back and made me giggle when he commented,

"Mmm minty."

"What can I say, I am obviously a girl prepared for anything."

"Are you prepared to start the day as I had planned." I smiled at this, beaming up at him before nodding.

"Great, time to get your sexy ass up then!" he said, pushing off the bed and shocking me as he started to walk away. Of course, the sight of his naked body wasn't exactly helping with that request.

"Oh…" I let slip, making him look back at me with a knowing grin. Then, just as I was pulling my feet up ready to get off the bed, he shackled my ankle and yanked me back down before covering me once again.

"But of course, I am teasing you," he exclaimed before running his nose up my cheek, telling me,

"Although, it was worth it for that look of disappointment, knowing now how much my girl needs my touch in the morning… *almost as much as I need hers."* He whispered this last part after making his way to my neck and up to my ear. I shivered against him and the grin I felt there against my skin, told me he didn't miss it. But then again, he didn't miss anything.

"I miss you when I wake and find you have slipped from my grasp," he said reading my mind.

"You looked deep in sleep," I told him as he shifted to one side of me so his hand was free to start exploring beneath my robe.

"Mmm, must have been lost in my dreams of you," he replied and again, I made him chuckle when I mouthed the word,

'Smooth'

"I do try," he said, making me moan when he plucked at a pebbled nipple.

"You do succeed," I told him in return, before moaning again when he rolled the hard bud between his fingers. Then he yanked at the robe so my waiting breast slipped free and he could replace his fingers with his mouth instead.

"Oh God!" I cried, arching my back when he used his teeth. Then his hand slipped down my belly and as soon as he came close, my legs fell open of their own accord, making him chuckle around my nipple.

"Someone is eager," he commented, making me reply,

"Says the man with his hands down... Ooohh..." I ended this in a cry of pleasure, one that was followed by his cocky reply,

"Make that..."

"...With his fingers inside you."

CHAPTER 23
UNFORGETTABLE MOMENTS

The start to the day was perfect, and I lost count of how many times Ward made me come. Although, the ending was definitely the highlight. Especially when he took me from behind, using a hand to collar the front of my throat for some of it, and wrapping my hair around his fist for the rest. It was such a dominant hold on me that I came screaming long before he did, his dirty explicit words just driving my need to come higher and higher.

Growling down at me, how addictive I was, how he ached to be buried deep inside me, to watch me come around his cock was the fucking hottest Gods be damned thing he ever saw. I swear, trying to concentrate on getting ready after this was made even more difficult when Ward couldn't keep his hands off me.

But he could also see I was eager to go outside and explore. And well, seeing as he told me his business wasn't needed until later tonight when we were meeting back up with Anders to form a plan, it meant we had the whole day together.

Our second chance at a first date.

And my first time in a different country too! Needless to

say, I was excited, and he knew it as he spent the whole time I was getting ready smirking to himself. What did surprise me, however, was the packed suitcases full of brand-new clothes, all in my size.

"Where did all this come from?" I inquired after I had asked him if I would get too hot in the sweater I had worn here. He had motioned to the case in the closet and told me to open it.

"A shop most likely," Ward replied with a wink.

"Funny, but I don't remember a trip to the mall in between getting kidnapped and my first flight." I saw his face lose all humor before he pulled me by my rope belt, and growled down at me,

"Please do not remind me of that, not even in jest."

"Okay fine, but if I don't joke about it…"

"You will just forget it ever happened?" he tried, making me give him a pointed look, before I conceded. But this was also after he pulled me even closer and whispered over my lips,

"For me, please." My response was to kiss him, a reaction he seemed pleased about.

After this we showered, separately this time as I reminded him that if we did it together, then we would never end up leaving this room. Although, when Ward walked out after me, dripping wet with only a towel low on his hips, I instantly regretted the decision. Something he knew too, the cocky bastard, as he chuckled to himself.

I tried to ignore this God of a man sharing the same space as me, and concentrated instead on dressing. I had picked a summery yellow dress with white embroidered flowers, the top was strappy and it had a floaty skirt that swished around my knees. A pair of white strappy sandals on my feet and a sweep of my hair in a high ponytail, completed the look. As for Ward, he too went casual, with a pair of jeans and light-gray T-shirt, that clung to every muscle I just wanted to go back to exploring. His chuckle told me he knew this too.

"Come on, beautiful, time to show you the sights." I swear I almost squealed with excitement, and Ward knew it as he seemed just as eager as me. But then, at the dinner we had, before it all went to utter shit, thanks to Gomez, the uber asshole, he had talked about the places he wanted to take me. Which meant that I wasn't surprised by his enthusiasm. Although, he had never mentioned this particular place, I was buzzing all the same. Yet in truth, half of me hadn't believed it would ever happen, and now here I was, walking out into a whole new place in Europe, a place I had always wanted to be brave enough to travel around.

"Hola, buenos dias," Ward said to one of the staff as we passed, making me ask,

"What did you say?"

"I told her, I'm having a great morning as I fucked you good and hard only twenty minutes ago." At this I gasped and joked back,

"But you only said three words." At this he threw his head back and burst into laughter, not caring who stopped to stare at his outburst. He tucked me close, kissed my forehead and told me,

"I said, hello and good morning."

"How many languages do you know?" I asked next, making him raise a brow down at me, then cryptically told me,

"Many." Then he slipped his sunglasses down from his head and with my hand in his, he led me from the hotel straight onto what looked like a stunning promenade. One lined with beautiful palm trees, colorful bedded plants and fancy old-fashioned street lights that I knew would make this place look magical at night. But as for the day, one look toward the end of the promenade and it looked as though it simply met with the sea.

"It's beautiful," I said, making Ward grin.

"This is known as the Paseo, Balcón de Europa, or also known as the Balcony of Europe." I turned to look at him and then back at our hotel, which was literally perched right on it. It was also clear that it was the focal point of the town, and I wasn't surprised considering it afforded magnificent views up and down the coast.

"Come, let me show you," Ward said, squeezing my hand and walking me up toward the large arch that gave you the most incredible panoramic views.

"If you look left, down there, you have Calahonda beach and its neighboring coves, this is followed by Burriana beach and, in the distance, see over there, that is the picturesque village of Maro," Ward told me, holding me from behind and extending his arm out in front of me so I could easily follow his finger.

"Maro?"

"It is the site of the Nerja Caves, the ones I told you about," he added, making me react by sucking in air.

"The portal to Hell, how could I forget?" I muttered, making him laugh.

"And who might this fine fellow be?" I asked, referring to the life-size statue that was wearing a suit and had been positioned so he looked as though he had just stopped during his afternoon stroll and paused to admire the view. He was even leaning a hand back against the railings and he was currently getting his picture taken with one woman draping her arms around him, posing with him as if he was her date.

"Ah, now that is King Alfonso XII, who lived between1857 – 1885, I believe," Ward told me, impressing me with his knowledge of history, but then again, I suppose he had lived through it, so he would know a lot.

"He was king of Spain from 1874 to his death and was the son of Isabella II."

"Wow, it's like dating a history professor," I said, making him smirk.

"So, tell me something interesting about him," I prompted, because I didn't want him to stop.

"What, more interesting than the fact he was King?" he asked, making me nod.

"Alright, let me think," he said, making a show of tapping his lips as I could see he was teasing me.

"How about this, he went into exile with his parents at the time of the revolt of the Carlists in 1868 and was educated in Austria and England. I believe his mother abdicated her rights so he could be proclaimed king. However, he would only hold the throne just over ten years before he became a victim of the cholera epidemic of 1885." I swear my mouth opened in shock before I slapped the back of my hand to his stomach and said,

"Holy shit, how do you remember all that? Jeez, Ward, but you could write a book!" At this he laughed, grabbed my hand and drew me in.

"On what, how to impress cute little tourists I want to get in my bed?" I blushed at that.

"Oh, you know exactly how to get me into your bed..." I paused long enough to look him up and down before adding,

"And it has nothing to do with history lessons." At this he growled low and pretended to nip at me before whispering,

"Behave Siren, or you will soon find yourself learning a new lesson."

"Umm, and what's that one called?"

"What happens when you sexually tease your Enforcer," he growled, making me grin and wink at him before I continued walking. We made our way to the large, round center of a raised platform at the end, and I looked down at the floor to see a star. Again, I felt Ward's arms come around me from behind and soon his hypnotic voice was telling me stories close to my ear, making me shiver against him.

"You know there is a local urban legend that says that if you stand in the central circle of the star, just where you are now, you may make a wish and then your wish will come true." So, I closed my eyes and did as he said I should…

I made a wish.

After this we left the Paseo Balcón de Europa, walking toward the town that I could see was lined with cafés, restaurants and ice cream parlors and with the beautiful sun shining, it was a hive of activity. We walked around its quant little streets, which was full of interesting little shops, selling things that I tried not to show too much interest in as I knew Ward would just be tempted to spend money on me. But inside I was practically itching to go in and discover all the wonders.

As for the town, it seemed filled with whitewashed narrow streets just like I imagined it would be, all brimming over with potted flowers blooming in every color and thriving under the hot Mediterranean sun.

But I started to notice that as much as I was in awe of my surroundings and staring at everything there was to see, Ward's eyes were nearly always on me. Like his enjoyment didn't come from the culture or the scents of delicious food, but instead it came from seeing me enjoying it all. So much so that when we finally stopped for something to eat, I couldn't help but ask,

"I take it you've been here many times before." Ward didn't even pick up his menu, because it was as if he knew what was on it, and what he wanted. This was another clue, but then he surprised me.

"Once or twice but I hardly remember either time to be honest."

"Oh my God, but how could you ever forget a place like this! It's beautiful." Which was when his reply shocked me, as he gave me an intense heated look before telling me,

"I won't be forgetting it now."

CHAPTER 24

FAMOUS LAST WORDS

"*I won't be forgetting it now,*" he said, and I was unable to miss the intense way he said it. Which was why I asked,

"Why, has it changed a lot since then?" At this he whispered my name, in sort of a gentle reprimand.

"Eden."

"What, did I say something wrong?" I asked naively. At this he chuckled lightly and shook his head before telling me,

"No, Eden, but ask yourself why I would remember it now and not before," he said, making me reply,

"Oh... OH... you mean me?" At this he laughed again and reached across the table to tell me,

"Yes you! Gods, Eden, there is only ever you." At this I blushed and the moment the waiter came over to take our order I tried to pull my hand back, but Ward just tightened it, making his point. He would let go of me for no one.

"I haven't read the menu yet," I said feeling my cheeks heat.

"Do you mind if I order for you, I think you will like tapas." I nodded letting him, as I had no clue.

"As long as there isn't…"

"An anchovy in sight, yes I remember." He winked, making me grin.

"Dos Gambas Pil-Pil, Patatas bravas, Carne con tomate, croquetas de pollo y Tortilla de patatas y dos tinto de verano, gracias," Ward finished, making the waiter nod before taking our menus and leaving.

"Wow, impressive again, of course I had no idea what all that was."

"Then it's food that also comes with a surprise," he replied smoothly.

"And what you ordered at the end, I think it was drinks?"

"Tinto de verano, it means summer wine and is different to local sangria, but I think you will like it." I laughed and held up my hands and told him,

"Hey, you had me with wine." This made him laugh and I was starting to get addicted to the sound. We continued talking about the place and he told me about the little white church we had passed before coming this way.

The Church of El Salvador was a lovely little building situated on one edge of the Balcón de Europa and close to what Ward told me used to be the Guards Tower.

"It was beautiful, but then this whole town is," I told him, taking a sip of my drink as they had not long been put on the table and mine was already half gone. It was delicious.

"It was erected in 1505, although the existing structure was not built until 1697, and was then further extended at a later date."

"I seriously don't know how you remember all this," I commented with a shake of my head. But Ward just shrugged his shoulders as if it was nothing and before I could ask more, the food started coming out. It was all on little plates so we could try a bit of everything, and I liked the look of it all, yet it was the sizzling prawns that I loved the best.

"Man, but I will not be forgetting those prawns in a while!" I said, patting my stomach and making Ward chuckle as we walked away from the restaurant, one that had overlooked the sea.

"They are a favorite of mine too."

"Ah, so that's why you ordered two plates, that makes sense now… note to self, Ward doesn't share food and gets possessive over prawns… gotcha," I said, pretending to write on an imaginary piece of paper. This made Ward laugh again, before he pulled me close, tipped my chin back and said,

"There is only one thing in my life I am possessive over and will never fucking share… *you.*" Then he kissed me, making me melt against him.

Once lunch was done, we continued to walk hand in hand back to the main area and I got excited when I saw all the ice cream choices, making him laugh when I tugged him over.

"Tutti Frutti for me, no, wait, mint choc chip… with sprinkles… oh wait, I can't decide!" I said, making Ward laugh.

"If you do not choose soon, I will be tempted to buy you the whole…"

"Strawberry please!" I shouted quickly, making Ward chuckle behind me.

"I will have the same… erm, minus the Sprinkles." I had to giggle at this and still had the urge to laugh when we took our desserts and started to walk back along the Balcón de Europa, near our hotel which was opposite.

"Would you like to walk down to the beach? It's a lot of steps but quite beautiful down there." The moment he said this, I faltered in my step and felt a pain in my chest.

"Eden?" I didn't know what to say so I only thought of one face in my mind, telling him silently that I wasn't ready. He frowned for only a split second before an understanding tenderness overtook his features.

"Second thoughts, the view from up here is far better, let's find a spare bench." I grinned huge at him and squeezed his hand tighter in mine, grateful that he didn't make me say the reasons why.

"So, tell me more about this amulet, why is it so special?" I asked, licking up my ice cream and making Ward stare at me when I did.

"Focus, babe, it's ice cream not... erm, the place I haven't been to yet." His eyes grew wide before a beaming grin took hold of his perfect kissable lips.

"Now, I am only going to focus on one word in that sentence."

"Yeah, which word is that?" I asked before purposely licking up it again.

"Yet!" he answered making me blush.

"Now keep teasing me like that and I will be tempted to toss the ice cream and take you back to the room for another kind of dessert." I giggled at this and then pretended to protect my ice cream before taking a huge unsexy bite and making my point, one that made him laugh.

"In answer to your earlier question, I believe it's an Astrological Sigil."

"Erm, a what now?" I asked being totally clueless.

"Depending on what is transcribed and what symbols adorn it, in its most basic form, I believe it to be a key."

"A key?" I repeated.

"An amulet as ancient of this one, with the Sigils it holds infused within the rock and metal it's made from, it makes sense."

"Why does it make sense?" I asked, wondering if my questions were about to get annoying. He put an arm around me and gave me a squeeze at this thought, telling me that I wasn't.

"It is Hell in nature, whereas most Sigils of the modern world present a different thing, some a method of healing, more so than to previous amulets found, ones that harness the force of the stars and magic for cure or protection, that sort of thing. Of course, this has always just been mortal belief, that objects can be utilized as a form of healing. Yet in my world they are used for much more," he told me, making me wonder what the one he had found was used for if it had originated in Hell.

"Where did you say you found it again?" At this question he looked grim and for a second, I didn't think he would tell me.

"Gomez had it on him," he admitted, making me gasp.

"Now what was that asshole doing with something from your world?" Ward gritted his teeth and said,

"I don't know but I intend to find out."

☖

"Come, we will be meeting Anders for a drink shortly," Ward told me once we were back on our feet and my ice cream had been long ago consumed.

"Should I change?" I asked, making him chuckle.

"No, you are perfect just the way you are… besides, if I get you alone again, we most likely won't make that drink." I couldn't help but grin at this, loving how easily I could turn him on or how much he wanted me.

"Always," he whispered after hearing my thoughts. Then he took my hand and ordered softly,

"Come, let's go find a table." My grin was his answer as he started to lead me toward a cute little square next to where we had bought the ice creams. It looked like it held apartments above as the buildings around were tall, creating a welcoming shade from the hot Spanish sun, even if it was only September. As for the ground floors, these were taken up by different types of restaurants and bars, everything from Mexican, Chinese, Italian and of course, Spanish. The delicious smells filled the air but after all our food at lunch and the massive ice creams, I was glad we were just going for drinks.

"If we are hungry later, we can…"

"You know you are going to have to teach me how to turn it off at some point," I interrupted, making him pause, and then he grinned down at me and said in a knowing tone,

"Now why would I do that, when it gives me so much insight into the way you feel and see the world… when it gives me so much pleasure?" I wasn't sure what to say to that, because as nice as it sounded, I also knew that my thoughts could potentially be the only private thing about me.

"Eden, I…"

"Ward and his lovely Eden, I am pleased to see you both looking so well rested… I hope you have enjoyed your day sightseeing?" Anders said when he spotted us walking over. He was sitting outside like most of the chairs and tables were, with only fewer tables inside. Something I was starting to realize in Spain was the norm, and no doubt due to the gorgeous weather.

"We are having a very pleasing day, my friend, and one much needed for us both," Ward replied, taking his hand and shaking it.

"Now that I can understand, as Deke brought me up to speed in our meeting," Anders replied as he was about to hold a seat out for me, when the look Ward gave him must have had him thinking twice. Instead, he chuckled and bowed his head, saying,

"But of course." This was when Ward placed a hand on my lower back and guided me into a seat, one he held out for me, making me smirk at his possessiveness. Some would have felt it as being too much but for me, it was nice to feel cared for and protected. I felt a squeeze on my thigh at this thought, before he leaned into me and told me quietly,

"Sweet thoughts indeed." I blushed at this, knowing he was referring to my earlier complaint about him still being able to read my thoughts.

"Now tell me of the caves," Ward said, turning his attention back to Anders, who had made a motion for the waiter to bring us the drinks he must have ordered.

"I have had my people clear the area of tourists, so it will be ready for your inspection, My Lord."

"Good, I will go there tonight and…"

"Tonight?" I interrupted in a panicked tone. Ward picked up my hand and told me,

"The sooner this is done, the sooner I can get you home." This didn't comfort me.

"But will it be dangerous?" I asked, making Anders cough once, trying in vain to hide his reaction behind a fist to his mouth. As for Ward, seeing as he still had my hand in his, he squeezed it and told me,

"There is nothing to fear, Little Carino." Anders cleared his throat and added,

"Besides, there is no rush, the site was all clear when we checked and like I said, there is time yet and…" Anders was suddenly cut off by the sound of screaming. Not just any screaming, but a sound so horrifying, I knew instantly that it couldn't have been human.

It was however…

A Demon.

CHAPTER 25
WORSHIPING THE MAKING UP
WARD

"You were saying?" I said the moment our next problem presented itself and started crawling down the side of the buildings. Anders and I were up out of our seats the moment I heard the unmistakable sound of a fucking Harpy!

"I don't understand, how did this happen?" Anders said in astonishment as all the people around us started to panic at the horrifying sight of one of Hell's beasts. Harpies were hideous winged creatures that were another creation of Zeus', and ones damned and forgotten about the second he got bored with them. But it was once said that they had started off life as beautiful beings. However, after they had been cast down to Hell, as they descended further through the layers of each realm, they lost more and more of their beauty with each gasping breath. What remained was what I was seeing now.

They looked a bit like giant birds that had lost all of their feathers, and what remained were wings that were nothing more than stretched, worn and pitted skin between long, gnarled fingerbones. Its naked body between these wings looked half starved, with a protruding ribcage, pronounced hip bones, and a pair of sagging breasts that looked covered in paper thin skin that had even torn in some patches.

"We are going to need crowd control here," I ordered, gritting my teeth as I sent my Darkness forward, capturing the Harpy while it was scrambling up the wall, trying to use the metal grates over the windows as leverage. It howled the second my power touched it, lassoing its leg and preventing it from going anywhere. Not until I had the chance to send it back to where it came from.

I instantly stood in front of Eden, protecting her before reaching out to Deke with my mind, who had been shadowing us all day. Not that Eden noticed, just as I had wanted. I hadn't wanted her to know that I had back up at the ready, just in case, something it seemed I was right in doing.

Deke was there in seconds, coming to stand next to me and creating more of a barrier between the Harpy and my Siren.

"Anders, get your men on crowd control, make sure no mortal minds make it through."

"I started the barrier, but it won't hold," Deke told me, making me glance back to see every human that had witnessed this Harpy attack now standing in a zombie-like state, unmoving near the entrance to the square.

"My men will take over it, should it start to break," Anders said, nodding now to his men who had all been situated around different restaurants in the square.

"Good, in that case, Deke, take Eden, get her to safety..." At this my girl gasped.

"I'm not leaving you!" Eden shouted, making me growl back at her as soon as Deke tried to lead her away and she fought against it. My Demon erupted and snarled at her stubbornness.

"Obey me!" She flinched back at the sight of my anger, but

it was too late, the Harpy had broken free of my restraints and took to the sky, making me roar in rage,

"TAKE HER, NOW!" I tried to reach out again for the Harpy, as I had done in the beginning, only this time she flew too high. I released my wings, fully intent on reaching her, when suddenly she took a different direction, tilting her wings, so she would fall to one side. I growled in frustration at her defensive maneuver, one that kept her just out of reach, when my heart started beating faster seeing now where she was headed.

"NO!" I roared when I saw who she had in her sights,

"EDEN, GET DOWN!" I bellowed out the warning, as she had slipped free of Deke for a second time and was trying to make her way back to me, the foolish girl. I was fucking furious as much as I was panicked, as I could see her getting closer. Which meant that by the time she landed on top of her, I was only close enough to grab hold of her leg with the longest stretch my Darkness could reach. I could see the Harpy snapping her large rows of teeth over Eden's face, looking as though she wanted to take a bite right out of her.

I suddenly yanked back, drawing my Darkness tighter into my body now we had a secure hold, making sure to drag her back enough so Eden could squirm her body from under her. I watched as the Harpy dug her talons in the ground either side of her, leaving deep gouges in the stone, letting me know this could have quite easily been done to my girl's flesh.

I finally got close enough that I was standing over the Harpy, keeping her locked in place by my Darkness that was at great enough strength to overwhelm her in my hold. Then I bent and took a taloned hold of her neck in my Demonic looking hand, raising the squirming Harpy in the air. I used my other hand to lock back her wings that were trying to knock me to one side so she may get free again.

This was when I looked down at Eden, who had only managed to get about a few feet away but was still on her back on the floor. She flinched at the dark look I gave her before I snarled,

"Get. Out. Of. Here... NOW!" At this dangerous demand she quickly scrambled to her feet, just as Deke stormed over and grabbed her.

"Do not fail me again!" I barked at him, before turning my attention back to the creature at hand. It snapped its overly long jaw at me, with its mottled skin turned a deeper shade of red, a color that matched its slanted crimson gaze. It shrieked at me the moment I slammed into a wall, using my growing talons to cut off the sound, as the threat to rip out its throat was obvious.

"You will pay for trying to take her from me!" I growled dangerously, making her eyes widen for a moment.

"I would not hurt her... not another child of the damned... damned by Zeus... another cursed and victim of our father." It grated out in a voice that barely sounded as if it had been used in years.

"Then you have something left of a soul to send back!" I snapped before plunging my Darkness into her body, impaling her with spears of my power. Enough to consume the very essence of her so I could deliver her quickly back to Hell. She bellowed out a haunting scream before it died off into a silent howl with her jaw now hanging slack.

I pulled back my Darkness, letting her body drop to the floor as it had already started to turn to ash, having no need for a vessel now her soul was detached.

"Now where the fuck did she come from?" Anders asked, coming to stand next to me.

"I don't know but I have a fucking good guess!" I snapped before walking away and checking on the progress of damage control.

"You think the portal in the caves is…"

"Open. Yes, I do, and I have a fucking good idea who opened it!" I snapped, feeling my rage still lingering, and most of it was admittedly aimed at Eden. My Siren, who could have gotten herself fucking killed! Oh yes, I was fucking furious!

"Then we must do all we can to close it," Anders said, making me turn my dark gaze on him and say,

"Not we, but I will be the one to do so, as only I hold the key, but right now… *I have a Siren to reprimand.*" After this I walked away with unspoken assurances that Anders would clean up this mess. This left me free to storm my way back into the hotel and up to the top floor the suite was on. I swear, by the time I threw open the door I was shaking in my anger, a feeling that was only cooled slightly to see my girl pacing the floor with tears in her eyes.

A feeling that was doused in ice the moment relief took over her entire body as she closed her eyes and looked up to the ceiling, whispering her prayer,

"Oh thank you, God." Then she ran straight to me and threw her arms around me, making me take in a deep breath, as though she was my lifeline and the very source of oxygen I needed to live.

"I was so worried!" she told me, crying into my neck, and I could do or say little but hold her there. This was when I noticed Deke sigh before rising to his feet and walking over to us.

"She's been a mess, no matter how I tried to reassure her," he told me, making me grit my teeth and nod, as right in that moment, it was all I could do to prevent myself from tearing him a new asshole. And one look at his face and he knew I was pissed off, which was why after another sigh, he left.

"Are you alright?" she asked me, which was when I hit my

limit, now detangling myself from her hold on me, gently forcing her to let go.

"I am fine, just as I knew I would be," I forced out without looking at her, putting distance between us.

"Ward, you're not invincible here, anything could have…"

"What!? Anything could have happened? You're right, Eden, it could have, but it wouldn't have happened to me!" I snapped, making her flinch before sighing herself.

"Look, I know you're angry but…"

"Oh no, I am not angry, Eden, I am fucking furious!" I growled, making her jerk back again before her soft, pretty features hardened as she became defensive. She even crossed her arms over her chest, and I tried not to focus on the way it lifted her beautiful breasts. I swear, the sight made my fucking mouth water!

"Do you have any fucking clue what that thing could have done to you!?" I snapped, making her say,

"But it didn't."

"Yes, because I was there to fucking stop it! I was there, Eden! Me! The one whose job it is to send these fucking things back to Hell! Not you… *me!*" I shouted this last part, and I could see she hated seeing this side of me and fuck me, but the unshed tears in her eyes told me she was seconds from crying. A fact that felt like fucking acid in my veins, but then I knew this was needed. It was a necessary evil that I had no choice but to punish her with. Because I couldn't allow her to act like that again. I couldn't allow her to put herself in danger again.

She was too important to me.

Which was why I had to be this hard on her, despite hating every fucking second of it!

"Yes, I get that, Ward, trust me… I am just fucking human and useless, right!?" she threw at me, as if being human was an insult, making me tense.

"That is not what I said!" I snapped back.

"No, but you didn't need to as it's there, written all over your face!" she said, making me growl.

"But you are fucking human, Eden, and it's not fucking helpful when I not only have to save you from fucking monsters, but first from your fucking self!" I roared, making her actually take a step back this time.

"Well, let me help you out then!"

"You can't fucking help me, Eden... wait, what the fuck are you doing?!" I asked the moment she reached for a lightweight jacket out of her suitcase and pushed her arms through with angry, jerky movements.

"What does it look like I am doing? Leaving, is what!" she answered with her own growl of words, before storming out of the room.

"What the fuck just happened?" I asked myself, before I bolted after her out of the door. I caught up with her easily, wrapping my arms around her so as she couldn't take another step away from me.

"You're not leaving me!" I snapped, making her tense in my hold before she said,

"Fine, what else would you suggest I do to make life easier for you, Ward?" she bit out, making me growl.

"Tying you to my fucking bed again, that worked the first time!" This was the only warning I gave her before I spun her around and pushed her up against the wall, kissing her. She pulled back and slapped me, now panting like some wild kitten cornered and scared. But then my Darkness started to seep through and instead of backing away, she grabbed me by the shirt and kissed me this time. I actually gasped in shock, even more so when she started pushing me against the wall opposite, as if she had a plan on where she wanted me.

Then she reached around me and soon the wall disappeared behind me, giving way to a room.

"Oh look, we did find a broom closet after all," she said, winking at me before pushing me against a shelf and kissing me again. Good Gods, but my little Siren was utterly insatiable! Her little hands were everywhere, tugging at my clothes and getting impatient making me chuckle, having clearly lost this argument.

"Easy, little one, there is no rush." At this she looked up at me giving me wide innocent eyes that danced with mirth and mischief, and I was soon to find out why.

"Eden?" I questioned for half a second before she started to lower to her knees in front of me. Then, while keeping my gaze locked at the fucking gorgeous sight of her, she said,

"You were saying?" Then she yanked open my belt with such force, I jerked to the side. I swallowed hard at how fucking sexy her actions were, unable to say I had ever experienced anything like it before, as I had always been the one in charge. But this... fuck me, this was something else!

It was fucking hot!

She took hold of me, and I swear I was fucking lost to the raptures of this little Siren and the first swipe of her tongue. By the Gods, I was ready to become her slave! She had teased me long enough with that fucking ice cream and now, for the first time in my fucking long life, I actually had to force myself not to come too soon. The urge to explode all over her talented little tongue was almost too much to bear! Just like the urge to fist her hair and force her to take more of me, to push my cock down her throat and make her gag around it. Gods, she was fucking perfect, I knew she would take it so beautifully for me. But right now, for her first time doing this to me, I didn't want to worry her or make her regret her decision to pleasure me this way.

And besides, I may not have been getting my entire cock inside her hot little mouth, but what she was doing was nothing short of fucking cock worshipping, as I swear, I was in fucking Heaven!

"Gods! So fucking good… that's it, so good, Eden, keep at me, baby," I cooed, and the moment I did, she was encouraged to take me deeper all on her own. At this, my hands slammed into the shelf behind me, just to stop my fucking legs from collapsing as I could see now she had just been teasing me.

"Fuck! Fuck, fuck, fuck… Eden, Gods woman!" I said, panting through my pleasure and again, it was becoming too much to hold off, as the second she started bobbing her head over me in earnest, I lost it!

"Fuck baby I am going to… going to… AHHH!" I roared out my release, trying to first to give her a warning so she may move her head but no. Not my insatiable little Siren.

She swallowed me whole.

Every. Last. Fucking. Drop.

CHAPTER 26
A SIREN'S SCREAM
EDEN

After this, I licked my lips, loving the taste of him bursting across my tongue and the power I felt from the act. His fingers caressed down my jawline and under my chin before he gathered up what I must have let spill from my lips as he pushed it back in my mouth. I sucked his thumb, stroking the taste off his skin and making his eyes glow amber with the sight. Then he pulled it from me, and before I could mourn the loss, I was picked up from under my arms and turned, so I now sat on a workbench that looked to hold stacks of individually wrapped toilet rolls.

"I'm going to fuck you now," Ward growled, which was my only warning before he tore my panties to one side and thrust up inside of me, making me cry out in shock.

"Hottest fucking thing, that tongue of yours!" he told me as he powered into me, making me cry out as I knew I wasn't going to last long. Not after the sexual kick I had from sucking his cock the way I had.

"Show me that tongue… give it to me!" he demanded and at first, I felt a little embarrassed about sticking it out, but knowing that was what he wanted, I did as I was told. He

203

grinned down at me, before taking it in his mouth and sucking on it like I had done on his dick. It felt so dirty, so carnal, it drove me higher, before he tore my jacket down my shoulders, bringing my arms tighter together at my back where the material caught.

"Hands," I moaned after pulling back from his brutal kiss, but his grin came before he twisted my jacket, making it tighten around my wrists.

"Now why would I free you, especially when I have you exactly where I fucking want you!" he snarled, thrusting up inside me even deeper that time and with his hold on me, this was when he started fucking me even harder, making the whole fucking room shake.

"Ahhhhh!" I screamed as my first release ripped through me, before it was quickly being chased by a second one.

"Ward… God… yes! Fuck! FUUUUCCCKKKK!" I roared as I shuddered around him, before he too came a second time, spilling himself inside of me with a roar of his own. It was a good job too, as I was close to losing feeling in my hands as I let my body sag against him, too exhausted to do anything else. Then, without a word, he pulled himself from where he was still hard inside me. Then after tucking his erection back in his jeans, he lifted me up into his arms, before carrying me back to our room.

"Please tell me the fight is over," I murmured as he lay me down on the bed, kissing me on my forehead softly.

"Please tell me you will never put yourself in danger again."

"I will see what I can do," I replied with a smirk, making him groan.

"I mean it, Eden. Promise me, next time you will do as I ask." I swallowed hard at his stern tone and knowing that he needed this, I placed a hand to his cheek and said,

"I am sorry I didn't listen and yes, I promise you, next time

I will not put myself in danger." He released a relieved sigh at that before whispering,

"Thank you," over my lips.

"Where are you going?" I asked when he looked to be getting ready to leave. He was standing at the wall safe, in the middle of retrieving the amulet wrapped in the cloth. I saw his back tense before he turned around to look at me but in doing so, the cloth revealed a little of the large coin, making him suddenly drop it with a hiss.

"What happened? Are you okay?" I asked, not used to seeing Ward be affected by anything.

"I am fine, it just slipped," he said, bending quickly so he could recover it and put it back in his pocket.

"Did it... *did it hurt you?"* I asked tentatively. At this he frowned for a moment as if he was trying to figure out how to answer that. When in the end he just... *didn't.* No, instead he simply headed toward the door and said,

"I have to go."

"Wait! Where are you going?" I asked in a panicked tone, making him release a heavy sigh before turning back to face me.

"Get some rest, Eden, and I will be back by the time you wake... *I promise."* I didn't have time to reply, as the sound of the door shutting made me jump. But by the time I got off the bed and ran to the door, I looked down the hallway, only to find him...

Gone.

After this, I knew I had no choice but to do what he suggested, getting some sleep, doing so in hopes of passing the time quickly enough that he would be there when I woke. *Just like he promised.*

I was actually surprised when I was able to sleep, feeling myself falling quickly. However, it was where my dreams had taken me that was what confused me the most and yet, should I have really been surprised?

Naturally, I had never been to the Cave of Nerja before, yet I knew what I was seeing now was exactly how they would look. A man-made walkway and staircase that would lead tourists safely into the jagged cavernous space that looked about as close to walking into Hell as one could get. Ceiling, floor, and walls, there were every type and size of Stalactites and stalagmites imaginable, making it almost look like you were journeying into the mouth of some gigantic sea creature, and these were the rows of teeth you first had to pass through. Great mighty columns of rock were the width of cars, some big enough they would make a house look small.

But by being here wasn't the only reason my dream was strange, and suddenly I felt as if I had become a ghost in it. As if I was an outsider just being granted a small window of time to become a silent witness. I knew this when with a thought, I was transported down to where I saw a group of men standing around one of the rock formations. In fact, what was most strange about this one, was that it rose up from the ground like a person, as if there was a young woman shrouded in material, hiding all her features, leaving just the shell.

"Bring the girl!" one of the men said who remained hidden in a cloaked hood, just like the rest of them. There were four in total, with all of them wearing black cloaks that all held a symbol I couldn't make out on the chest. In fact, I would have only been able to make it out had they each pulled the sides of their cloak together, but as it was each cloak was open. It did however make me wonder if these men were part of that ancient auction house Ward was telling me about?

This thought soon left me when I heard a girl screaming. The sound echoed so loud I would have covered my ears had my body been real. However, the man in the middle, the one seemingly calling the shots, simply laughed before the girl was close enough for him to backhand her across the face. She went tumbling to the ground, spitting out blood as her head hung down, making me automatically reach out and try to help her.

However, my hand floated right through her, making me gasp. But before she had a minute to compose herself, the hooded man grabbed her by her dark hair, wrenching her head back painfully and making her cry out.

"Now it's time to use that sweet Siren voice of yours, just like I showed you."

"I… I… can't… I told you… it was a mistake… I don't…"

"Then your friend is dead."

"No! Please, no!" The hooded man pulled a phone from his jacket and showed her a picture, one I couldn't see but whatever it was, it made her start to cry.

"NO! Please, oh God, please don't hurt her! I will do it, I will do whatever you ask me to, just let her go!" At this he let go of her hair and pushed her into the stone that looked like a covered woman.

"Then fucking do it!" he snapped, making her gasp, a hopeless sound that was as though someone had ripped a sob from her. She fell to her knees at the base of the stone woman and this time, she raised her shaky hands up in front of her.

"It's time, men, protect your ears, for I doubt you are all worthy of possessing one of her kind," he said, lifting his hands to his ears and casting what seemed like some kind of spell. The others did the same, just in time for the poor girl to open her mouth and this time, when she screamed…

It literally tore open Hell.

I knew this the moment light erupted from the center of the stone in front of her, and soon she wasn't the only one who screamed when a Demonic hand shot out from the crack.

"AHHH!" The girl bellowed in fright as suddenly the same

amulet was then placed in her hand, as if the Devil had been the one to give her this gift. She screamed one last time before falling backward and passing out, still with the amulet clutched to her chest.

"She did it!" one of the other men said, his shock being obvious.

"Of course, she did," the man in charge said leaning down now to caress her red cheek like he actually gave a shit about her.

"Now all we have to do is be ready to capture whatever gets drawn through," another man said, making the one in front reply,

"Leave that to me."

"And the girl?" his friend asked, nodding down to her.

"Put her in the next auction, I have no more use for her now other than the money she can bring me, for I have a feeling she will bring me a pretty penny."

"I would fucking say so, Gastian, she's a fucking Siren, people will pay millions," another said, making me try and recall the name.

"Yes, millions that fucker Warden Za'afiel stole from me!" he growled, making me suck in a startled breath, as this was the man he called his enemy.

"Speaking of the Enforcer, what will you do to prevent him from trying to close the portal?" one of them asked, before the other sounded even more worried about the idea of Ward showing up, asking,

"Yes, what do we do if he turns up and tries to shut it down?"

"Let him," Gastian said in a dark tone, making me frown, wondering why he would go to all this effort if that was what he would allow to happen.

"But why?" One of his men asked this very question, however, his answer only made one of us gasp silently.

"Because he will die trying, that is why."

"But nothing can kill that son of a bitch!" the others complained.

"Not true, for there are plenty things in Hell that can kill him, after they first drag his Angelic soul through the portal that is!"

'NO!' I screamed this time, and the last thing he said had me waking, gasping for breath before the screaming started. Because what I just learned, Ward didn't know.

The very last thing Gastian had said before I got sent back to my reality.

One that had quickly become my...

Nightmare...

"Only a Siren can close it."

CHAPTER 27
DESTINATION SAVE ASS

Deke quickly ran into the room the second he heard my screaming, which was a good thing as it would save time.

"Edie, what the Hell happened?" Deke asked as he found me bolting up out of bed, and when finding me in just my underwear, he turned quickly as if someone had promised to pour acid into his eyes should he ever look at me sort of naked.

However, I didn't have time for that shit right now, which was why I snapped,

"Hell happened... now quit that crap as we don't have time for it!" Then I started dragging my legs into a pair of jeans, because I figured it would be cold in a cave. That poor girl had looked cold for damn sure. God, but I hope we weren't too late to find her either. One thing at a time, Edie.

"Okay fine, Ward can punch the shit out of me later for looking, but right now, can you tell me why you're putting your T-shirt on backward?" he asked, making me roll my eyes before I whipped it off again and started to do it right this time. Then I grabbed my socks and sat so I wouldn't fall over.

"Eden!" he snapped, making me stop for a second, before telling him,

"You have to take me to the caves." At this it took two seconds before he swiped a hand down and said firmly,

"Oh, fuck no, not a fucking chance!" At this I sighed before pulling on my last sock in an angry motion that I was surprised didn't break my toes.

"You have to!"

"Why?" he snapped.

"Because he is in danger and he doesn't even know it!" At this he threw both hands up and said,

"Oh, not fucking this again!" This was referring to spending the entire time I waited for Ward to come back with him convincing me that he was fine. But no matter how much he told me what a hard ass Ward was, I still couldn't stop myself from worrying. But this was different. This was not that time.

This was serious.

"Look, honey, I told you, Ward is going to..."

"DIE!" I shouted back at him, making him frown down at me, as if he was only now just starting to take me seriously.

"Okay, so I am going to be as blunt as I can here, because I don't have time for anything else. Ward thinks that he can close a portal into Hell with this amulet he found."

"Yes, okay so we are on the same page with that one."

"Yes, but this is where that book gets fucked, Deke, as that is precisely what Gastian wants him to think." He jerked back a little at this before narrowing his gaze.

"How the fuck do you figure that?" I scrubbed a hand down my face and told him the part I didn't think he would believe.

"Because I just had a dream of when it all happened. He used a Siren to open up the portal and when his men asked what would happen when Ward turned up to close it, he laughed and said to let him."

"Fuck! That slimy little fucker!" he said, surprising me by believing this to be true, and even after I said this was all from a dream.

"Come on, we've got to go!" he said, taking my arm and leading me quickly from the room, making me need to practically jog to keep up with him. Not that I cared as I would start sprinting if it was needed.

"Please tell me those caves aren't far."

"Lucky for you, I know someone with a fast car," he replied, winking down at me.

֎

"Please, I beg of you be careful with her," Anders said as we both lowered ourselves inside the beautiful sleek supercar, one that I knew my step-dad would have drooled over. An Audi R8, and utter beast of a car and well, like Deke had said, we would need it!

"Hey, just think of it like this, if I scratch it, then you know who to send the bill to," Deke said with the window down, and poor Anders looked as though he had just handed over his first born for us to take joyriding.

"Not funny, Deke," he replied, making Deke chuckle and wink at him before putting it in gear and wheel-spinning it out of the private parking lot Anders had used.

"So, what's our play here?" I asked, making him grit his teeth before releasing his tense shoulders with a shrug.

"Fuck if I know!"

"That doesn't exactly give me the warm and fuzzies here," I told him, before needing to hold on as he took a roundabout with speed, something I was most definitely not used to seeing in the States... Jesus, but whose idea were these things, someone with a death wish!

"At least we know now how Gomez got that fucking amulet."

"What do you mean?" I asked, holding on again before swinging back in my seat until I was straight.

"Think about it, Gastian wants Ward to go to the cave, needs him to go there thinking he can close this portal, one he only knows about after finding Gomez trying to use this amulet against him." I sucked in a deep breath,

"What do you mean he used it against him... what can it do to him?" I asked, as it was clear Ward hadn't been the most forthcoming with me about everything that had happened.

"It's a powerful conduit forged in Hell, so for our kind, an Angel like us, it would drain him of his power, making him weak, say..."

"Say fighting against a bunch of Demons trying to claw their way through a portal... okay yeah, I get it now... doesn't this car go any faster!?" I asked, freaking out and making Deke grin at me once before telling me,

"Hang on." I did as I was told and held the fuck on, caring not for the ride, only the destination...

One that meant Life or Death.

CHAPTER 28
LAST WORDS
WARD

The moment I got to the caves, I wished I had left things between us differently. I should have told her what the amulet did to me, but I didn't want to worry her. Gods, but I couldn't wait until this was fucking done with, so I may finally take my girl home. Because as enjoyable as the day together had been, it only made me more eager to get her back to Italy. So that days like earlier continued and weren't in fact tainted by obligation and duty.

I just wanted to start our lives together.

I pulled the amulet from my pocket, one I made sure to keep covered this time, and growled down at my hand. I just needed one fucking thing to go right for once as I had a promise to keep. A promise to be there when she woke up and I would be damned if I broke it because of something as simple as closing a fucking portal. Although, I had to confess, I was uneasy about this one, as it was only ever supposed to be a myth.

Oh, but there were plenty of unused portals over the world, but they usually died out from lack of use, and therefore lost the power to maintain them. Because an active portal was only powerful when it was used, as it gained power each time by taking that essence needed for the exchange. Therefore, it made no sense that an old, unused portal like this should even have any power left, being that it should have died out long ago. But then, if this was the case, how had that Harpy got through into the mortal realm?

Well, I would soon find out, I thought, rolling my shoulders as I made my way inside the entrance. It was one typical to find at a place like this, as ever since its discovery on the 12th of January 1959 by a group of young locals, it had been opened as a tourist spot. Locals who had been on a late-night walk searching for bats of all fucking things.

Well, something told me I was going to find a lot more than fucking bats, that was for damn sure, as I could even smell the Demonic essence lingering. It was clear now that the fucker Gastian had been using this place as his own personal fucking goldmine, and the Gods only knew what he had already ripped from it, ready to sell. But then, was I really surprised? Especially considering I had financially crippled him. But then I knew that he had wanted this place long before. This plan of his had been in the making for a long fucking time, he was clearly just waiting for something.

Now the biggest question was, what?

Why would he have needed to open a portal again? It wasn't like adding fuel to an engine and turning on a fucking switch. I frowned to myself as I continued down inside, ducking at the lower parts and just waiting for the chance to release my wings and fly down there.

"Fuck!" I hissed when the largest part of the cave opened up, and the first thing I homed in on was the now man-sized gaping tear in the realm's unseen barrier. It was what protected any realm, only there were always weak spots in the space between two. It was why there weren't many portal points left,

as the King of Kings had most of them all shut down thousands of years ago.

But this wasn't like any portal I had ever seen before, as it looked unsteady, and volatile. As if its means of being there had been forced by hatred and pain. As if the person calling forth the magic needed had been unsure of their powers and had been forced into acting, doing so on fear.

"What the fuck happened here?" I asked myself as I walked closer, seeing the white woman who had once guarded this cave. Before now she had barely been anything more than the eroded figure of a person, watching as mortal after mortal passed her on the path that had been created. Years and years of passing judgement on each, doing so silently as their souls were read like scripture.

However, now she was a stone figure of a weeping woman on her knees, holding her frozen hands to her chest, one that looked as if it had been torn open and had her heart taken. Her face cast down as if expecting to see the blood of death overflowing onto the shroud that covered her slight frame.

It was a haunting sight, made even more so by the portal that was glowing angrily behind her. A swirling mass of darkness that started to pulsate the moment I realized something else was trying to push their way free.

"Not today, fucker!" I snarled before stepping up to the white woman, the keeper of the caves, and without touching the amulet, I reached out and tried to place it inside. However, what I didn't expect was the echoing sound of pain to come screaming from the woman as she lifted her head up and let go of the most horrendous sound of death. The force of it sent me flying backward as the amulet flew from her chest toward where I had landed.

"No! It... it can't be... possible?" I said, after hearing the

217

sound of what any Enforcer blessed by the Fates would recognize…

The desperate call of a Siren in pain.

Of course, this didn't give me long to think, just enough time to act as all of a sudden, a pair of Demonic arms appeared, after being thrust through the opening. Then, once there, they took hold of the portal, a sight that looked more like them taking hold of nothing but air. Then once they had hold, they started to drag the rest of their body through, making me realize this was a much bigger problem than I first thought.

Which was why I got back to my feet and the moment it made its way through, I said,

"Alright, asshole, you want to dance? Let's fucking dance." Then I called forth my Darkness and for the first time in my entire existence in the mortal realm…

My Darkness didn't answer.

CHAPTER 29
WORST NIGHTMARES

The moment the creature finally dragged itself all the way out, I was still trying to will my Darkness to appear, knowing I couldn't fight this Demon with nothing more than the fists of my mortal vessel and without a weapon.

"Oh fuck, an Oni... fucking perfect," I muttered when the monstrous being stood to its full height, one that towered over me at seven feet tall. I walked over to one of the nearest stalagmites and snapped it off at the base, meaning I now had something to fight with. Although, how well it would hold up against this big bastard, I had no clue.

An Oni was depicted as an ogre-looking Demon in Japanese folklore. Oni were mostly known for their fierce and volatile natures that centered their evil souls on feeding from murder and cannibalism. Whether they were the ones to carry out the act or forced others to do it for them, it mattered not. This hulking great figure was also as ugly as they came, with its cracked, crimson dark skin, horns that made up most of the foreheads and overdeveloped upper and lower canines, it gave them one hell of an overbite.

They were dumb fuckers too, so I could use its stupidity to my advantage here. They also only relied on their center eye that was above their nose and appeared to be sideways, always making me wonder if it saw this way too. Well, not that I gave a shit, for it could die with the world upside down for all I cared, as long as it died quickly. As for its other eyes, these were milky white and utterly useless as they were blind.

It sniffed the air and jutted out its overly long chin, before snarling my way when tipping its head to the side so it could see me better.

"Well, I guess that answers that question," I muttered before rolling my unconventional weapon around trying to get a feel for the fucking thing. Then it threw its thick arms back, ones with chains still dangling down from its thick wrists, before running straight at me. The thing looked as if it had just escaped from somewhere, making me wonder what fucker was just on the other side of that portal playing puppet master?

I didn't have long to think on this before I was dodging his attack, making one of my own in return. I jumped to the side and threw myself off one of the rocks, using it to gain height so I could slice the jagged end of my weapon down its back, making it howl with pain before it caught me in the chest with a swing of its arm. I flew backward and smashed into the cluster of stalagmites, feeling my body need to fix itself as I forced myself up to standing. I snarled down at one of the stalagmites that had broken off in my side, making me curse as I yanked it from my vessel.

"Fucker will pay for that one," I vowed with clenched teeth, before throwing it aside. It would also pay a lot fucking sooner should my powers decide to hurry the fuck up and come back to me. Speaking of the asshole, it reached up and grabbed one of the biggest stalactites growing from above and threw it at me. This meant I was left dodging something the size of a fucking table, as it smashed into the cave wall behind me, making pieces above rain down from the impact.

I picked up my fallen weapon and decided to take a different approach, but then after trying to call forth my wings and nothing happened, I knew the advantage of height wasn't on my side either.

"Fuck!" I snarled again as it came charging my way. It must have been the amulet, acting like some kind of conduit for my powers, being amplified in here. Meaning there was no way I could fight with my Darkness as long as I remained in here.

I dodged another hit, watching as the dumb fucker ran into the wall, which was when I finally got an idea. I looked around for the best place I could find to make it most effective and ran toward it. Then, knowing what was at my back, I whistled, gaining its attention once more.

"Yeah, you, fuck me but it looks like your mother fucked a blind goat!" I shouted, making him roar at me before doing the exact thing I knew he would... he charged.

"That's it... a little more... a little more... there!" I shouted, throwing myself out of the way at the very last second, which meant the dumbest fucking Demon in the world just ran into a wall of spikes and ended up impaling himself!

I released a sigh of relief as the thing started howling in pain, before I could use my weapon to stab it in the back of the neck, killing it instantly. However, when I heard the same roars I knew it made, was when I realized my problems were far from over.

Because this wasn't the only Oni that had made it through.

No, now there were two more.

"Fuck!" I hissed, and something told me that before this night ended, it wouldn't be the last time. It also looked as if I wouldn't be keeping my promise after all, that was...

If I made it back to my Siren at all.

And that was when Fate just wanted to kick me in the balls, as soon, the roar of an Oni wasn't the only sound echoing in these caves.

"Please Gods, no."

"WARD, LOOK OUT!" Eden's scream froze my veins instead of getting me to move like she had intended, however, she hadn't come alone. Deke grabbed me out of the way just before I was knocked off my feet by the next charging Oni.

"What the fuck is she doing here!?" I snapped, grabbing him and growling an inch from his face before we both pushed apart and started fighting, trying to take care of these next two threats. Deke was the same as I, trying to call forth his powers, which meant when he punched the Oni, it didn't quite have the desired effect he was hoping for. So when the Oni hit him back, he went flying backward, landing at my feet.

"Yeah, tried that already." He groaned and forced his jaw back into place before getting to his feet again.

"You might have wanted to start with that," he commented dryly.

"What do you think I am doing here? Testing my abilities as a man for shits and giggles?" I snapped, before snarling at Eden as she tried to make her way to us. Was she fucking crazy?!

"GET OUT OF HERE!" I roared, before being tossed to the side when one used its horns to take me clean off my feet.

"Why the fuck did you bring her here?!" I growled the moment I was back on my feet and this time, I swung my weapon, cracking it across his face enough that it stumbled. Deke followed suit, breaking off a piece himself and using it as a weapon, slicing across the Oni's chest and making it howl in pain.

"She has a plan!" he shouted back to me, making me actually stop as my mouth dropped.

"Tell me you're fucking joking before I kill you!" I

snapped, making him shrug before ducking out of the Oni's arms as he tried to grab him. Then Deke slipped under his reach and hammered his Stalagmite over his back, driving him to his knees. However, before he could deliver the killing blow, it pushed all of its weight back, running backward until it crushed Deke against the wall, pinning him there.

"Deke!" I shouted his name, dodging my own Demon before charging at the one ready to turn around and attack my friend. I ran toward it and at the right moment, kicked up from the wall Deke was against and speared the fucking thing in the center eye. It dropped dead instantly, and I offered Deke a hand to pull him from the spikes of rock that had imbedded into his back.

"Well, that wasn't fucking fun."

"You will find yourself back there if she gets hurt!" I snapped before trying again. "So help me, Eden, if you do not fucking run…!"

"Just keep that fucking thing busy!" she snapped back at me when she made it to the ground level, and as soon as I saw the thing start her way; I knew I had no fucking choice than to fight it so it couldn't get to her. I snapped another Stalagmite from the floor, this one thinner, and I started running for the thing, shoulder barging it the second I was close enough. This took it out of Eden's path, who looked to be running toward the white woman. But I didn't have chance to get to her, as I leapt on the Oni as soon as it was down, stabbing it in the side of the head, knowing taking out the neck or head was the only way to kill these fuckers.

"Oh shit!" I heard Eden's panicked voice before she looked back at me with wide fearful eyes.

"Where is the amulet?!" she shouted, looking around frantically, but this was the last of our worries as I saw the long brown tentacle coming from out of the portal and it was headed straight for her.

"NO!" I roared, running for it, and getting there just in time to knock her out of its way, meaning that instead of her...

It got me.

CHAPTER 30

A SIREN'S HEART
EDEN

"NO!" I screamed when I saw that spiked brown tentacle reach out and grab him. It had wrapped itself around him and was now trying to drag him back toward the portal and my fear had never felt so great. I had never felt so fucking scared of anything in all my life than I did in that moment, watching as the man I loved was being dragged toward Hell.

A Hell I knew he would never survive.

But he looked at me, even as the tentacle was wrapping itself further around him, tighter and tighter. It was closing up around his head now, and his eyes told me so much. They told me the very last sight he wanted to see was me, finding it with the evidence of my pain and anguish pouring down my face in tears that wouldn't stop. He had saved me, sacrificed himself for me. Something he was still trying to do with his very last moments on Earth. He called out to me, telling me the only thing that mattered to him,

"Run... run... Eden... please, my love... live for me!" I closed my eyes for only a second, cursing the fact that I couldn't find that fucking amulet. That I didn't have the power

to stop this! That I couldn't save the day or the man I loved the way I had hoped. The way I had counted on. Deke was still trying to force his broken body to move, trying everything left in him to get to his friend.

But it was no use.

It was unbearable. This pain of losing him a second time, being made to watch as he was being dragged away from me. I couldn't do it again. I couldn't bare it.

"No!" I shouted, and then just as the last of his eyes disappeared from view, I screamed louder,

"No!" But then as I felt something happening all around me, I welcomed it instead of shying away from what it could possibly mean. I didn't let fear get in the way, I just held onto my anger and fury. I hung on to my need for vengeance and fear. I hung on to what I wanted and suddenly, I knew how to get it. So, I opened my mouth and this time, the sound that came out was one that belonged only to a Siren who was calling out to her Enforcer.

"I SAID NOOOOO!" I roared, screaming so loud that it shook the entirety of the caves, and I heard the agony of Deke behind me. But it wasn't just his pain I heard, as the wailing cry of whatever creature had Ward in its grasp could also be heard, feeling my fury. It dropped its hold on Ward just before it could drag him inside, and his body fell to the ground. The sight only angered me more, asking why he hadn't yet moved. So I screamed even louder, feeling the weight of my love for him crushing down on me, knowing his death would kill me!

"GET UP, ENFORCER!" I bellowed, making parts of the cave crumble around us, knowing that if I didn't stop soon, we would all be buried alive regardless.

'Give me back the heart of the cave.' This voice startled me as it seemed to be spoken directly in my mind and suddenly, I looked to see the statue of the woman had started

to move her head and hold out her hands, as if waiting for me to do something. So, I held my hand out behind me and cried out again, knowing that this time I was calling for her heart, the piece of her that had been stolen, just like it had in my dream.

I sighed in utter relief when I felt the cold disk fill my palm and before a second of time could allow more of those creatures through, I thrust my hand into the open cavity of her chest and screamed...

One last time.

This was enough, as it not only made the stone woman's wound close around it, but it also fractured the portal. A sight that had me crying out in fear as the once swirling abyss of darkness started to change, until a blinding light burst from inside. I ran over to Ward and threw myself over him, trying to protect him from whatever was happening.

I buried my head in his chest, holding on tight until whatever was happening stopped and soon, the sound of my frantic panting was heard.

That and the sound of Ward's heart beating.

"Ward?" I lifted my head up and looked down at him, placing a hand to his cheek, letting my tears fall onto his skin.

"Come on, babe, please just open those handsome eyes for me," I begged, crying now, something that turned into a sob of relief as his lids fluttered open.

"Oh, thank God!" I shouted, throwing my arms around him and crying uncontrollably now. An emotion that intensified when I felt his arms curl around me and hold me to him.

"Eden?" His groggy voice spoke my name, making me pull back enough so I could look down at him.

"You... you saved me?" he asked softly, making me suck back my sobs enough for me to tell him,

"You saved me first." At this he grinned, and the sight

managed to fix all the pain at seeing him being taken had caused. It was the most beautiful sight I had seen in my life.

Because he was my life.

I felt that down to my bones and the very core of who I now knew I was.

His Siren.

CHAPTER 31

OBSESSED

WARD

Being back at Afterlife only days after all that had happened between myself and Eden wasn't exactly where I wanted to be. I was still in a state of shock that she had saved my life. But then if the stories were true, then that was always as it was fated to be, that a Siren was supposed to save the life of her Enforcer, I just never really trusted it to be true before that night.

Thankfully, Deke had also survived the force of Eden's Siren, a powerful being that would no doubt only grow after the summer solstice but until then, I was determined to start our lives together. Something that could only truly begin after I had met with my King and told him all that had happened.

Yet even now, knowing that she was back at the hotel where I had left her being protected by Deke, it still grated on my soul to be parted from her. Even despite claiming her many times since the first time, it didn't ease the desperate need to be with her, but only strengthened it!

I was a man obsessed, I knew this!

It made me wonder, would I forever be this way and if I was, did I even really give a shit to change? I loved my Siren and she loved me, that was all that mattered. That, and the news of what Gastian had done. I had already been here an hour and spoken to Dominic Draven in his office. We had agreed to allow the fool to believe the King knew nothing so as he wouldn't be any the wiser when the rest of the Enforcers were called to Afterlife for their yearly meetings.

Then the King would deal with him.

And I would fucking be there!

But as for now, well it was time to take my leave and get back to my girl. My obsession. However, as I approached my King, now being back in his club, I knew that I wasn't the only one who felt this way about another. I could see it for myself, even without the mortal being visible, and someone his gaze seemed riveted on. His tall, imposing figure was standing by the VIP's balcony edge, overlooking his club below, or should I say, looking at a single mortal girl who looked to be working behind the bar.

"A new waitress?" I questioned as I approached, making him grin in a way I knew meant he had plans for her, and perhaps this included committing his own abduction.

"Indeed, and an intriguing one at that," he replied, making me smirk as I thought back to my own intriguing beauty I had left purposely exhausted in my bed. Fuck me, but she had cried out my name so beautifully and gave new meaning to the name Siren and paradise.

"I came to inform you of my departure, my Lord," I told him, making him acknowledge this with a nod.

"You believe her to be the first of the lost Sirens then? You must if you're willing to take such a risk," he said, making me tell him honestly,

"She is worth every risk and much more."

"Yes, that I can understand," he replied with a distinct glow of his dark eyes flashing purple.

"My Lord?" I questioned to see if he would elaborate or not.

"Some mortals just have that power over you," he commented, fisting the railing and making the metal beneath his hand bend and almost crumple under his strength. Well, this I could most definitely agree with, for I had most certainly been bewitched by my own.

"Isn't that the fucking truth?" I admitted with a gruff sigh and a rub of the back of my neck, making the King laugh.

"Very well then, go and take your lost Siren with you, if that is who you believe her to be."

"I do, my Lord, and I think, given the circumstances, timing would add strength to my claim, or perhaps I speak out of turn," I commented, nodding down at the pretty girl.

"You do not," he admitted, telling me in that moment just how much he trusted me as one of his Enforcers. As I doubt he would have admitted as much to another, unless on his council and even then, I knew at least one who he would keep such information from…

The bitch, Aurora.

"But such knowledge goes unspoken until I have claimed her… *do you understand?*" he said, adding a Demonic edge to this order, and I recognized that same caution in my own tone when it came to my Eden.

"But of course, my Lord, for I would never betray such trust." He nodded at this and went back to looking at his little mortal. A girl, it had to be said, who was a delightful creature, if not a clumsy one, as she banged her hip against the counter for the second time since this conversation began. I held my countenance as I watched the King wince and fist his hand, as if pained by being unable to go down there and save her from… well, herself.

"Then I bid you good luck and will take my leave," I said

after another moment of silence passed between us, as it was clear his thoughts were elsewhere and centered solely around a blonde beauty. One who had just dropped a customer's change, making the King's lips twitch in amusement.

"Any advice for me?" he suddenly asked, making me take pause.

"Truthfully?" He nodded, making me answer with honesty.

"Kidnapping seems to work well enough." At this he laughed, and I could quite honestly say it was not a sound I had heard often, if at all.

"I will keep that in mind," he commented with a knowing grin, as if he had already thought of it and was just biding his time.

"That is wise," I answered in jest, making him smirk as I moved to leave once more, eager to be back to my own little captive.

"Oh, and Ward, do me a favor..." he said, pausing only for a moment when tearing his gaze from the girl so he could issue me this warning by looking me in the eyes.

"Until the summer solstice when you can prove your instincts correct, I suggest if you want to continue to indulge in the forbidden mortal fruit, then do so discreetly."

"My Lord?" I questioned, already knowing what was coming after hearing something similar from him only days ago.

"I like you, Ward, and would hate to be forced to make an example out of you when others start to take notice and wonder why I haven't yet extended that same law to you," he said, making his point.

"Understood, my King," I replied, knowing to take his advice seriously as this was a free pass if ever there was one, and I was smart enough not to parade it around and take advantage of it.

"Good, now go and enjoy her, for I soon hope to do the same with my own," he said, looking back down at his own mortal fruit, one not forbidden to the King, as it was clear he had finally found his own Fated One. Something he confirmed when he spoke as if she had the power to hear, now looking up at him from below and no doubt seeing the same darkness in him that Eden had found in me that night.

A darkness ready to consume her.

His little unsuspecting waitress.

"Soon, my Chosen One, for your time of being unclaimed is quickly running out... and soon, there is no escaping your fate... *no escaping your King... not when...*

You're eternally mine."

EPILOGUE

EDEN

Weeks Later…

I stood on the balcony and looked out to the private beach, as I seemed to do every morning. I still hadn't yet made it out there, telling myself each day that I would. Ward knew this and yet, being as patient with me as ever, he told me to take my time. That he would wait for me. Because every morning he would get up first and go walking out there, after asking me to join him.

Every morning I had given him the same answer.

"Not today."

But I hadn't done that this morning. No, I had shocked him by saying okay, which was why he was still standing out there now, waiting for me. He had his back to the beach house, a holiday home, and one of many I was to discover after he finally got his wish and we made it to Italy. This had been after a quick trip back to the States so we could bury my brother, and also so he could speak to his King.

He had asked me why I hadn't told him about Jimmy as he held my hand at his grave. I had let the tears fall and told him,

"Because I felt ashamed."

"Eden?" He said my name but I couldn't face the words, so I thought in my mind for him to see it all for himself. Everything that happened that day, I just had to get it out… I had to set my mind free.

"You survived for me," he told me, making me suck in a shaky breath before admitting a second later,

"Not all of us did."

"What do you mean?" he asked, pulling back and now looking concerned at my tears gathering and ready to overflow.

"My brother… I had to watch… they… he… Gomez shot him," I told him in between my broken sobs, making him grab me and pull me into him, this time cradling my head to his chest as he soothed my ragged soul. He didn't say anything to this, but then again, he didn't need to. Because I knew how he felt. How anyone would have felt really. Jimmy had been the one to get me into this mess.

A mess that led me to Ward.

I couldn't be angry at that. Not when it felt like he had put me on the path to my destiny. Because I may not yet fully understand what a Siren was, but I was no fool. I knew it meant I was different in some way. I had seen that the moment my scream had closed the portal, had stopped that monster. Even back when my scream had stopped the man in the warehouse. The way Wrath had looked at me, as if finally discovering some ancient myth was true. As if the Fates had finally spoken and Enforcers had no choice but to listen…

Listen to their Siren's call.

But Ward understood the guilt I felt, even if I knew he didn't agree. Because the guilt of living my life and wanting it more than Jimmy was the only shame I felt, and when I looked at Ward, it floated away. My love for him was stronger than all else. That was why I knew I needed to let go of all of my guilt, not just what I felt for Jimmy.

But what I felt for my mother.

So, taking a deep breath, I stepped outside and down the few steps that would take me onto the beach. The first beach to feel my toes since my mom passed. Of course, Ward knew I was there, he always knew.

So, I simply stood next to him and without looking at me, he took my hand in his and asked,

"Are you ready?" I nodded, before putting my hand in my pocket and pulling free the plastic heart with its colored band I had made for my mom. The one I should have buried her with. Well, I was too late to do that now but this, we both agreed, was far better. I let his hand go after first giving it a squeeze and started walking closer to the water, letting my feet get wet. I closed my eyes and looked up at the heavens.

"Well, Mom, I finally got here. I finally made it across the sea." I let my breath catch before looking down at the heart in my hand, telling her, one last time,

"I miss you, so much. I wish you could have seen it with me, it's like we always dreamed it would be. I wish you could have seen so many things, but I have one last wish to make, and I'm sure you will understand when I tell you that he's standing behind me. Goodbye, Mom, I love you, forever and always," I said, crying before I threw the heart into the water, watching as it floated along the waves... as if she was there reaching for it.

"I heard that wish," he told me, stepping right up behind me and referring to the day in Nerja, when he told me about stepping on the star.

"Now it's time to tell you mine," he said, making me turn around to face him and this time, I gasped when he started

237

lowering to one knee. Then he took my hand in his and pulled out the box I remember him having in his hand in my dreams.

He flipped it open to reveal a stunning diamond ring and suddenly, my hands were shaking as he took one in his own, then he asked me,

"Eden, my little Carino, will you marry me and be mine forever?" I let out a gasp and before I knew it, I dropped to my own knees, and while the waves of my living dreams floated in around us, I put my hands to his face and told him,

"Yes, a thousand times yes, I will marry you, my Hero!" At this he grabbed me to him and told me with all the love in the world...

"Then wishes really do come true... for us both, my Siren."

If you would like to discover what happens when the King of Kings tries to claim his own Chosen One, his little waitress, then download your copy of...

Afterlife book 1
Available now on Kindle and Kindle unlimited.

ACKNOWLEDGEMENTS

Well first and foremost my love goes out to all the people who deserve the most thanks which is you the FANS!

Without you wonderful people in my life, I would most likely still be serving burgers and writing in my spare time like some dirty little secret, with no chance to share my stories with the world.

You enable me to continue living out my dreams every day and for that I will be eternally grateful to each and every one of you!

Your support is never ending. Your trust in me and the story is never failing. But more than that, your love for me and all who you consider your 'Afterlife family' is to be commended, treasured and admired. Thank you just doesn't seem enough, so one day I hope to meet you all and buy you all a drink! ;)

To my family...

To my crazy mother, who had believed in me since the beginning and doesn't think that something great should be hidden from the world. I would like to thank you for all the hard work you put into my books and the endless hours spent caring about my words and making sure it is the best it can be for everyone to enjoy. You, along with the Hudson Indie Ink team make Afterlife shine.

To my crazy father who is and always has been my hero in life. Your strength astonishes me, even to this day! The love and care you hold for your family is a gift you give to the Hudson name.

To my lovely sister,

If Peter Pan had a female version, it would be you and Wendy combined. You have always been my big, little sister and another person in my life that has always believed me capable of doing great things. You were the one who gave Afterlife its first identity and I am honored to say that you continue to do so even today. We always dreamed of being able to work together and I am thrilled that we made it happened when you agreed to work as a designer at Hudson Indie Ink.

And last but not least, to the man that I consider my soul mate. The man who taught me about real love and makes me not only want to be a better person but makes me feel I am too. The amount of support you have given me since we met has been incredible and the greatest feeling was finding out you wanted to spend the rest of your life with me when you asked me to marry you.

All my love to my dear husband and my own personal Draven... Mr Blake Hudson.

To My Team...

I am so fortunate enough to rightly state the claim that I have the best team in the world!

It is a rare thing indeed to say that not a single person that works for Hudson Indie Ink doesn't feel like family, but there you have it. We Are a Family.

Sarah your editing is a stroke of genius and you, like others in my team, work incredibly hard to make the Afterlife world what it was always meant to be. But your personality is an utter joy to experience and getting to be a part of your crazy feels like a gift.

Sloane, it is an honor to call you friend and have you not only working for Hudson Indie Ink but also to have such a talented Author represented by us. Your formatting is flawless and makes my books look more polished than ever before.

Xen, your artwork is always a masterpiece that blows me away and again, I am lucky to have you not only a valued member of my team but also as another talented Author represented by Hudson Indie Ink.

Lisa, my social media butterfly and count down Queen! I was so happy when you accepted to work with us, as I knew you would fit in perfectly with our family! Please know you are a dear friend to me and are a such an asset to the team. Plus, your backward dancing is the stuff of legends!

Libby, as our newest member of the team but someone I consider one of my oldest and dearest friends, you came in like a whirlwind of ideas and totally blew me away with your level of energy! You fit in instantly and I honestly don't know what Hudson Indie Ink would do without you. What you have achieved in such a short time is utterly incredible and want you to know you are such an asset to the team!

And last but by certainly not least is the wonderful Claire, my right-hand woman! I honestly have nightmares about waking one day and finding you not working for Hudson Indie Ink. You are the backbone of the company and without you and all your dedicated, hard work, there would honestly be no Hudson Indie Ink!

You have stuck by me for years, starting as a fan and quickly becoming one of my best friends. You have supported me for years and without fail have had my back through thick and thin, the ups and the downs. I could quite honestly write a book on how much you do and how lost I would be without you in my life!

I love you honey x

Thanks to all of my team for the hard work and devotion to the saga and myself. And always going that extra mile, pushing Afterlife into the spotlight you think it deserves. Basically helping me achieve my secret goal of world domination one day…evil laugh time… Mwahaha! Joking of course ;)

Another personal thank you goes to my dear friend Caroline Fairbairn and her wonderful family that have embraced my brand of crazy into their lives and given it a hug when most needed.

For their friendship I will forever be eternally grateful.

As before, a big shout has to go to all my wonderful fans who make it their mission to spread the Afterlife word and always go the extra mile. Those that have remained my fans all these years and supported me, my Afterlife family, you also meant the world to me.

All my eternal love and gratitude,
Stephanie x

ABOUT THE AUTHOR

Stephanie Hudson has dreamed of being a writer ever since her obsession with reading books at an early age. What first became a quest to overcome the boundaries set against her in the form of dyslexia has turned into a life's dream. She first started writing in the form of poetry and soon found a taste for horror and romance. Afterlife is her first book in the series of twelve, with the story of Keira and Draven becoming ever more complicated in a world that sets them miles apart.

When not writing, Stephanie enjoys spending time with her loving family and friends, chatting for hours with her biggest fan, her sister Cathy who is utterly obsessed with one gorgeous Dominic Draven. And of course, spending as much time with her supportive partner and personal muse, Blake who is there for her no matter what.

Author's words.

My love and devotion is to all my wonderful fans that keep me going into the wee hours of the night but foremost to my wonderful daughter Ava...who yes, is named after a cool, kick-ass, Demonic bird and my sons, Jack, who is a little hero and Baby Halen, who yes, keeps me up at night but it's okay because he is named after a Guitar legend!

Keep updated with all new release news & more on my website

www.afterlifesaga.com
Never miss out, sign up to the
mailing list at the website.

Also, please feel free to join myself and other Dravenites on my
Facebook group
Afterlife Saga Official Fan
Interact with me and other fans. Can't wait to see you there!

facebook.com/AfterlifeSaga

twitter.com/afterlifesaga

instagram.com/theafterlifesaga

Also by Stephanie Hudson

Afterlife Saga

Afterlife

The Two Kings

The Triple Goddess

The Quarter Moon

The Pentagram Child - Part 1

The Pentagram Child - Part 2

The Cult of the Hexad

Sacrifice of the Septimus - Part 1

Sacrifice of the Septimus - Part 2

Blood of the Infinity War

Happy Ever Afterlife - Part 1

Happy Ever Afterlife - Part 2

The Forbidden Chapters

*

Transfusion Saga

Transfusion

Venom of God

Blood of Kings

Rise of Ashes

Map of Sorrows

Tree of Souls

Kingdoms of Hell

Eyes of Crimson

Roots of Rage

Heart of Darkness

Wraith of Fire

Queen of Sins

*

King of Kings

Dravens Afterlife

Dravens Electus

*

Kings of Afterlife

Vincent's Immortal Curse

The Hellbeast King

The Hellbeast's Fight

The Hellbeast's Mistake

*

The Shadow Imp Series

Imp and the Beast

Beast and the Imp

*

The Lost Siren Series

Ward's Siren

Eden's Enforcer

Wrath's Siren

Emme's Enforcer

*

Afterlife Academy: (Young Adult Series)

The Glass Dagger

The Hells Ring

The Reapers

*

Stephanie Hudson and Blake Hudson

The Devil in Me

OTHER AUTHORS AT HUDSON INDIE INK

Paranormal Romance/Urban Fantasy

Sloane Murphy

Xen Randell

C. L. Monaghan

Sorcha Dawn

Kia Carrington-Russell

Sci-fi/Fantasy

Devin Hanson

Crime/Action

Blake Hudson

Mike Gomes

Contemporary Romance

Gemma Weir